THE CHOICE

ALLISON J. KENNEDY

Copyright 2014, 2015 Allison J. Kennedy

This work is licensed under a Creative Commons Attribution-Noncommercial-No Derivative Works 3.0 Unported License.

Attribution — You must attribute the work in the manner specified by the author or licensor (but not in any way that suggests that they endorse you or your use of the work).

Noncommercial — You may not use this work for commercial purposes.

No Derivative Works — You may not alter, transform, or build upon this work.

Inquiries about additional permissions
should be directed to: allisonjkennedy@yahoo.com

Cover Design by Maria Aiello

Previously published as *The Choice*, Booktrope Publishing, 2015
Previously published as *The Choice*, Astral Ink Publishing, 2014

This is a work of fiction. Names, characters, places, brands, media, and incidents are either the product of the author's imagination or are used fictitiously. Any resemblance to similarly named places or to persons living or deceased is unintentional.

*For the little ones.
Someday we'll see you again.
Until then, run wild and free with the angels like you.*

No rape story is typical. Everyone heals differently. This book is fictitious and should in no way imply that a victim should recover in silence.
Please see the acknowledgments page at the end of the book for information on how to report a rape, and for resources on getting support.

One

Now

SHE'S ONE YEAR OLD. She has so much hair. It frames her angelic face in golden curls, and I wrap them around my fingers as I sing her to sleep. Lights from the carousel on her dresser dance around her dim, peaceful nursery as I rock her. My heart aches as she nuzzles against my breast. This is love. This is peace. Each day she grows, she teaches me how to let go.

Then

IT WAS THE FALL OF 2010. A Friday. I remember the exact day because I remember how miserable the weekend was following it. My senior year at Ocean View Private School had just begun. Ocean View was the only private school in Newport, Oregon. Honestly though, I didn't understand what that particular school had to offer differently than the public one up the road, other than stricter studies and easier access to drugs. I mean, we were rich kids, after all. I never touched the stuff though. I avoided most recreational activities that might have made me "cool" to instead focus on my future. I wanted to be a doctor—a cardiologist, to be exact. And that's what I was trying to explain to Danika, but she wasn't listening.

"It's a lot of school, but I think it would be worth it. My dad thinks I should be a neurosurgeon like him though. I just don't think that's the right path for me."

"Mm," my blonde-haired, blue-eyed friend vaguely concurred while she scrolled through her text messages. She was leaning over her phone with her forehead in her palm like she always did during our lunch break. I learned long ago that I couldn't count on her listening when she was expecting a text message from Tyler Jenkins.

I sighed, watching her. Her highlights were fresh and perfect. She was wearing a new shade of pink lipstick. Her nails had glossy French tips. I always felt like she was supermodel quality, and she saw me as one of her style-starved spectators. I wasn't though. Her perfume was always stifling, and I preferred my Converse shoes over heels any day. "I've decided to skip college altogether and be a stripper," I said casually.

"Mm."

I tapped my fingertips on the table until she finally looked up at me, seeing recognition dawn in her eyes. "Wait, what?" she stammered.

I smirked. "I said I'm nervous about how many years of school I'll have to make it through. It'll be worth it, right?"

She locked her phone and tossed her hair over her shoulder as she shifted in her seat. "I think it will. You're smarter than anybody I know, so it shouldn't be too hard if you just take it day by day."

I brought my apple juice box to my lips and positioned the straw between my teeth while I evaluated her. Did she mean what she was saying, or did she just feel obligated to follow a compliment up with something cliché? I wondered why I was talking to her about this anyway.

"We'll see," I muttered around my straw, putting the box down without drinking. As I watched her return to her phone, I decided then and there that Danika, although she had been my friend for nearly a decade, was never going to be someone who cared much for other people's victories, defeats, hopes and dreams. She was incredibly sweet in that "girl next door" sort of way, but she rarely thought about anyone but herself.

I missed Addison, the third and final piece to our friendship triangle. She was the keystone that kept Danika and me supported. But she was in Italy, and without her presence, I was quickly learning how unstable my relationship with Danika really was.

"When is he going to text me?" Danika huffed and crossed her arms.

"Well, he's two tables away. You could go talk to him."

"He needs to take initiative, not me."

I stared at her manicure as I fought the urge to shut down her five-hundred-and-something'th rant about boys. Looking back, I wished I had. "I'm going to call my sister before class starts. See you there," I said, rising to my feet and slinging my book bag over my shoulder. I made my way out of the buzzing cafeteria and let the doors swing shut behind me, submersing myself in the rare delicacy of quiet halls. With a sigh, I walked across the sun-soaked, wood floor and stopped in front of my locker to turn the dial.

After opening it, I dug through my book bag for my cell phone. I tapped the first number on my speed dial and pressed the device to my ear. A clique of girls burst out of the cafeteria, chattering excitedly just as my house phone went to voicemail.

"Grace, it's me. Just calling to check on you. Are you there?"

I waited for a few moments to listen as I arched an eyebrow at the four sophomores who moseyed past me, making no effort to keep their voices at a reasonable decibel. Grace didn't answer. I sighed and began rifling through my locker for my biology textbook. "Alright, well, you might want to make sure you do the dishes or Mom will get mad. I'll check your schoolwork when I get home. Love you."

"Playing teacher?" a guy said behind me.

I put my phone back in my bag and turned around, meeting eyes with Tyler Jenkins. I glanced toward the cafeteria to see if Danika was hot on his trail. "Not really. Well, sort of. It's my little sister, Grace. She's homeschooled and my parents inducted me as her tutor." I turned my face back to him and noticed for the first time that he had flecks of green in his hazel irises. He was attractive, but not in a "pretty boy" sort of way. It was something else. He wasn't traditionally handsome; he just had this way about him. It was really no wonder Danika liked him, although I couldn't say much about his personality. I knew he was known for being a man slut.

"Your dad is my dad's doctor," he said, pushing his hands into the pockets of his slacks.

"I see." I nodded slowly. "Is your dad sick?"

"Seizures. Not too bad though. Just enough to interfere with his daily activities. He can't drive or anything. What I meant to say is that your parents seem to be pretty smart people. Couldn't your mom tutor her?"

I wondered how this was any of his business. I tilted my head, trying to decide if he was being rude or if I was just defensive. "My mom is a lawyer. She's pretty busy. Grace homeschools because she has trouble concentrating in groups."

"Gotcha," he nodded, rocking back on his heels. "That wasn't really any of my business. Sorry if that was rude."

I shrugged as I closed my locker. "No, you're not rude. I'm just protective, you know?"

"That's a good thing!" he said emphatically. "Actually, I saw you leave the cafeteria and I came to ask you a question . . . but that one just seemed to come out instead," he laughed, rubbing the back of his neck. "I'm having a party tonight. Nothing huge. Just thought it would be cool to eat lots of junk food and play dumb games like *Apples to Apples* and *Pictionary*."

"You play *Pictionary*?" I asked skeptically. The idea brought a smirk to my lips.

He threw his hands up in surrender. "What can I say? I'm a boring private school kid like the rest of us."

"What are you guys talking about?" Danika chimed sweetly, hooking her arm with mine in a way that always annoyed me. She looked up at Tyler and I didn't have to look at her to know her eyes were glistening like a doe in heat.

"How deprived we rich kids are," Tyler said with a note of humor.

"He's having a party tonight. Boring games and unhealthy food. You should go." I brought her up to speed as smoothly as I could without making it obvious that I was trying to tiptoe my way out of it.

Tyler tilted his head. "You should both come," he said with an almost genuine smile.

"Well, it's just . . . I have to help Grace with her schoolwork. And I don't really do big groups."

"It's the weekend, May," Danika said carefully, but her tone indicated something else altogether: a quiet demand that I comply because *that's what friends are for*. "You can help her tomorrow. We haven't done anything fun in months!"

"I thought horseback riding was fun."

"Oh, it was," she promised, but I knew she was lying. "But this way, we don't have to get dirty."

I almost rolled my eyes as I turned my attention back to Tyler. He was watching me expectantly and stiffly, almost like he wasn't giving me a choice. It wasn't hard to deduce that he didn't want Danika there.

And the thing was that if I didn't go, she would most definitely make a fool of herself. She would probably just end up crying all night behind the locked door of a bathroom. I knew enough about Tyler to know he wasn't the type to be pursued. He did the chasing.

"Alright, fine. I'll go. But we can't stay too late."

A crooked grin slipped onto Tyler's face and his eyes remained on me as he backed away. "Good. Seven o'clock. Just bring yourselves."

Danika almost squealed when he was out of sight. "Thank you, thank you, *thank you!*"

"You owe me," I grumbled. "And if this party turns wild, I'm leaving."

"Deal. I'll leave with you."

Yeah, I'm sure you will, I thought with a sigh.

* * *

"MOM?" I CALLED, shrugging my backpack onto the kitchen island. The house was quiet, so I figured she wasn't home at her usual time. I noticed a folded note next to the bowl of plastic fruit. Something was scribbled across the front, and I knew immediately that it was from my dad because I could barely read my own name. I unfolded it and sat on a stool.

May,

Your mom went to Portland for business. She'll be back tomorrow. I'll be home late. Call me if you need anything.

Dad

I rolled my eyes. At least I had an excuse not to go out. Dad would never let me leave Grace here at night. I left the note where it was to begin rummaging through the fridge. After grabbing a package of chicken breasts that I'd thawed the night before, I closed the door and paused to look at one of the only decorative magnets my mom allowed: a small laminated picture of our family, taken during a vacation in Maui. I was thirteen and Grace was eight. Dad's hair was still free of gray and Mom's boobs were two cup sizes smaller. Our smiles were all stiff and fake. We wore the same smiles we did in all of our family photos.

Next to this magnet was one with the hospital's logo on it. It held up another photo. This one was of me and Grace on our horses.

Grace and I had ridden ever since we were old enough to sit upright in the saddle. Same with Dad. So when we were born, it was only inevitable that we would be introduced to the lifestyle. I call it a lifestyle because when horses are in a person's blood, they're not a hobby or a sport. They're just a part of the rider. Dad had two, and Grace and I each had one. All of them were Quarter Horses, and all of them were bred to the hilt. But try as he may, Dad could never get me into showing for competition. Grace had already won several trophies in show jumping, and Dad's event of choice was dressage.

Mine? I rode for pleasure. Properly, I might add, since my dad had me in mandatory lessons until I turned sixteen in hopes that I would decide to show. He said I was a natural; that to not show would be a waste of my talent. I didn't see the logic in that at all. My talent made me safe in the saddle. It helped me explore different techniques. I could get on almost any horse and apply them, well trained or not. It made me happy.

Painting made me happy too. This was yet another hobby that might have seemed useless to some, but to me it was like breathing. Sometimes it was difficult to concentrate on my studies because all I wanted to do was sit behind my easel and create something new. Painting wasn't a way of losing myself like riding was though. It was a means of expression. It was a way for me to pour myself into something beautiful and freeing—something separate from the stiff life I had to lead. My parents were career-driven and strict. I should have thanked them for that, but it drove me crazy.

"Grace?" I shouted toward the stairs. "I'm home."

I began slicing the chicken on a cutting board while mentally preparing myself for the essay I had to write for my English class. Poetry had never been my thing, so I had retained very little in regard to what I'd learned about Dante Alighieri in the past. I was dreading it. I was also dreading the C I was inevitably going to receive for PE this semester. At least Christmas break was almost here. With that came obligatory family functions, stiff exchanges of affection, and the tradition of exchanging one gift between us on Christmas Eve, saving the rest for the next day. There was always so much chaos at my grandmother's house when it came to gift giving. How my mom had been birthed by this woman made no sense to me at all. She was always laughing, always welcoming, and always tipsy.

But I looked forward to the holidays because it meant two whole weeks of forgetting about school; two weeks to hide in my room or spend with my friends, to avoid the superficial things my parents enjoyed. I was sick of it all. College couldn't come any sooner.

I heard a door open upstairs and a moment later, Grace stepped into the kitchen. She looked like a miniature version of our mother, with her auburn hair slicked back into a perfect bun, and a royal blue sheath dress. Her silver kitten heels clicked across the hardwood as she approached the bar. I remembered she would be participating in a Spelling Bee this evening. "Hello," she said softly. "What are you making?"

I noticed a touch of gloss on her lips and sparkles dusting her emerald-colored eyes, and recalled the day that Mom started making me wear makeup. I never wanted to; it always made me feel dirty. Even as I stood at the stove in my designated school uniform of a plaid skirt and brown top, I knew I was a walking form of rebellion. I had skipped styling my hair though, which was the only choice I seemed to have in my daily attire. Mom wouldn't be home to see me anyway.

I placed the chicken in a pan with a bit of olive oil and seasoning. "Stir fry. Since when do you wear makeup?"

Grace sat on one of the stools, her back straight and her chin delicately lifted. "Since this morning. Mother said it was time."

"Of course she did," I muttered.

She blinked her enormous green eyes as if she was pondering my response, but said nothing.

I turned away and scrubbed my hands under the faucet. "Do you have homework?"

"No."

"Alright," I said with a sigh, drying my hands on a towel. "What's wrong?"

She looked at me and inhaled a long, slow breath. "I think I should speak with Mother about it."

I raised an eyebrow, crossing my arms. "Spill."

"I don't—"

"Mom won't be home until tomorrow, so I'm your next best thing." I rested my elbows on the kitchen island across from her, smirking deviously. "Do you like a boy?"

She didn't flinch. "I started my period last night."

"Oh," I gasped. Grace wasn't old enough to start her period . . . was she? I nodded reassuringly. "Do you want to talk about it?"

"No, thank you," she said, sliding off the stool. "I'm going to practice my music upstairs."

Her little heels clicked away as she strode toward the stairs, where she ascended them with a hand perfectly poised on the rail. Mom would be so proud.

I released a deep sigh and continued making dinner, deciding I would take some to her when it was done. The strains of Beethoven's *Fur Elise* trickled through the walls from above, careful and slow.

I fixed her a plate when dinner was ready, but I never got the chance to bring it to her because she came and got it herself. She whispered her thanks as she sat down at the dining table, her back to me. "What did you work on today?" I asked, taking my place across from her.

She cut a piece of broccoli in half and poked her fork into it without looking at me. "Math and social studies."

"Do you need help?" I asked. I pushed a piece of chicken into my mouth that was a tad larger than it should have been. I realized I was ravenous.

"No. I finished."

I chewed for a long time so I could speak. "Alright," I said, swallowing my food. Then I slipped my phone out of the pocket of my skirt and sent a text to Dani.

Me: Can't go tonight. Parents aren't going to be home and I can't leave Grace. Sorry!

I wasn't really sorry though. The last place I wanted to spend my Friday night was at Tyler Jenkins' house. My phone dinged and I glanced at the screen.

Danika: You can't be serious, May! I HAVE to go tonight! Please don't abandon me!

"Oh my God, you're such a drama queen," I grumbled, turning my phone over to ignore it. It just kept dinging.

Danika: May, please! Can't you find a babysitter?

"Hey, girls!" Dad announced. He stood in the front doorway, sunlight chasing him inside as he sat his briefcase down.
I shot myself with my imaginary gun as I typed another text.

Me: Looks like I'm coming after all.

Two

I HELD A COUPLE bobby pins between my teeth as I twisted my hair into a bun, pushing them into place to keep the unruly wisps in the front under control. I sighed at my appearance in the mirror. It wasn't that I wanted to dress up for this stupid party; I just couldn't remember the last time I wore something remotely pretty, and I wanted to make the best of it if I had to go. I spritzed my hair with hairspray and put the finishing touches on my lipstick before resting my hands on the waist of my simple green dress. The color made my red hair and green eyes pop.

"Going somewhere tonight?" Dad asked.

I slipped my feet into a pair of nude flats and looked at him. He was leaning against my bedroom door in his scrubs, his eyebrow cocked. "A board game party," I explained tepidly. "Nothing exciting. I promised Danika I would go."

"Will there be drinking at this board game party?"

"Nope." I smiled stiffly. "It's going to be pretty boring. No teenage drunkenness here, I promise."

He pushed himself off of my door frame and nodded, narrowing his blue eyes at me. "Alright. Be home by eleven. No later." He pointed at me with a stern look, but I knew him. Any time Dad was stern, it was a façade. Mom was the real rule enforcer.

"Eleven. Got it." I sighed as I picked up my purse. After digging my keys out of it, I brushed by him. He still smelled like the hospital. "Honestly, I doubt I'll make it that long."

"Well, have fun."

I glanced at my watch as I jogged down the stairs. It was already almost seven. I knew Danika would be squirming with anticipation and whining about my tardiness the moment I pulled up to her house, but she would live. I unlocked my Jeep and tossed my purse onto the passenger seat before slipping my key into the ignition. "You owe me, Dani," I muttered. I then backed out of the driveway, ready to get my friend duty over with.

* * *

TEN MINUTES LATER I pulled to a stop by the curb in front of her home. Danika was already waiting there in a short skirt and red cardigan, her arms crossed as she approached the door to pull it open. "We're going to be late," she whined in dismay, shutting the door. She sat her Coach bag in her lap and buckled her seatbelt.

"But fashionably so," I retorted, winking at her. "You look pretty, Dani."

Her annoyance seemed to melt away a little as her shiny lips softened into a smirk. "So do you. It's too bad Addison couldn't come tonight."

I doubt she would have wanted to, I thought. Addison and I were pretty likeminded on most things, including our distaste for juvenile social obligations. Just because people our age were expected to act like idiots, it didn't mean we had to. But if this party was going to be as tame as Tyler promised, then maybe it wouldn't be quite so bad. "She'll be home soon."

"I'm more than a little jealous of her, I have to say." Danika sighed as we merged into the flow of traffic. "Italy in the fall? Is that even fair?"

"I wish I could be there too, but I would say it's fair. She's earned it. I mean, her parents didn't give her a dime for this trip. It was all on her; all money she earned so she could go and explore the land of her heritage. I just hope she can make up her schoolwork."

"Pssh, what is schoolwork compared to Italy? Besides, she wants to be a dance instructor. That doesn't exactly require a 4.0."

Danika could sound so shallow without even meaning to. I sighed, flipping on my blinker to turn into Tyler's neighborhood. Everyone lived close together on this side of town. "It is if she wants to be accepted into her school of choice. By the way, where are you considering?"

"Cosmetology school," she shrugged, but then a grin broke out onto her face when she saw my disbelieving expression.

"You're kidding, right?" I gaped. "I mean, I have nothing against beauty school, but is that what you really want to do?"

"Of course not," she snickered. "But sometimes that's the only thing I think I would be good at."

"What about interior design? You've been talking about that for months now."

She flipped down the visor in front of her and smacked her lips in front of the mirror, fixing a minor smudge. "You have to be good at math." She closed the visor and eyed me with a sigh of dismay. "And we both know I'm not."

"You could be," I challenged. "You just don't try hard enough."

Her mouth fell open.

"I'm serious, Dani!" I looked at her as we turned another corner, taking us higher up the hillside of fancy lofts. "Nobody will give it to you straight, and that's why I do. Sometimes you play dumb and it's not very becoming."

"How do I play dumb? That's so mean!"

I pulled the car to a stop after squinting at the number on the front of a two-story, cream-colored condo. We were late, as we expected, but I took this opportunity to build Danika up in a way that nobody else would. "Look. You're beautiful—the most beautiful girl at Ocean View. And beautiful girls sometimes play dumb because that attracts attention from guys who think they can show them the ways of the world. But we both know you're not dumb. And honestly? When you act that way, I kinda want to punch you in the face. What kind of guy do you want anyway? Someone who just wants to use you and move on? Or someone who's attracted to that brain of yours, which we *both* know is fully capable of impressing without any effort?"

She blinked at me a couple of times and reached for the buckle of her seatbelt. "Whatever, May. I'm not a *genius* like you. And I'm sorry, but you won't attract anyone either unless you start caring about the way you look. Have you considered wearing mascara now and then?" she scoffed. "Let's just go inside, alright?" She pushed the door open and climbed out onto the sidewalk, slamming it behind her.

I pinched the bridge of my nose, stifling the urge to tell her how ridiculous she was being. I wasn't a genius. School was a struggle for me too. But Danika wasn't the type to listen to criticism in the moment. She would get angry, and then think about it later. I knew tomorrow she would be telling me I was right, so I turned off my car and got out to follow her inside. She was already halfway across the yard.

"Wait!" I called, but she didn't listen. I was beginning to wonder why I even tried to maintain a friendship with her. The door to Tyler's home was open and I could already hear the beat of thumping bass along with victorious shouts from a group of guy—probably over one of those board games Tyler had mentioned. But when I stepped inside, I saw that that wasn't it at all.

Jacob, a junior, was chugging down the foaming contents of a clear, plastic cup. A table was set between two groups, a short mesh net dividing it into two parts. I had seen this game in a movie one time: *Beer Pong*.

"Hey! You're here!" Tyler exclaimed, squeezing me into his side with one arm.

I moved away from him and pointed at the table. "Is this what you call a board game?"

He laughed a little too loudly. I could smell liquor on his breath. "Naw. The board games are in here," he said, steering me into the dining room with his hands on both of my shoulders. Sure enough, a few kids from school were holding up *Apples to Apples* cards, laughing hysterically. Shot glasses were strewn about, not a single one full. The whole place reeked. It smelled like a skunk had moseyed into the house.

"Where are your parents?" I asked.

"In Portland for the weekend! But don't worry, my dad already approved."

"Did you happen to mention the booze you would be serving?" I noticed a guy sitting at the table with a joint between his fingers. "And *marijuana*? Seriously, Tyler?"

He chuckled and draped his arm around me, holding his index finger and thumb very close together while he squinted at them. "I might have told a *tiny* lie about that part."

I tried to move out from under his arm, but he held me tighter. "Come on, May! Loosen up! Here, have one of these." He reached into his pocket and pulled out a tiny white pill.

I stared him in the eye. "What is that?"

"Just a disco biscuit, O'Hara! Do you *ever* pull your panties out of your ass?"

I shoved him off of me. "You're disgusting!" I snapped, looking in all directions for Danika. I exhaled in relief when I saw her.

"There you are!" Danika trilled. She stepped into the dining area then with her fist balled in front of her. Her eyes shifted from me to Tyler and instantly she lit up like a bundle of Christmas lights.

"What is in your hand?" I demanded.

"I found it on the floor. I thought maybe someone dropped their medication?"

I pried her fingers open and took the pill out of her palm, and then marched into the kitchen to toss it down the drain. When I returned, I was forced to pass through a cloud of pot, and Tyler was standing a lot closer to her than before. She had her bottom lip between her teeth, her eyelashes fluttering seductively. I grabbed her wrist and yanked her out of the dining room, but she put on the brakes. "What the hell are you doing?" she snapped, yanking her arm out of my grasp.

"That was ecstasy, Danika!" I hollered. At least, that was what I thought it was. I just knew it wasn't *medication*. "I told you if this party was wild, we were leaving."

"I don't want to leave. You're going to have to go without me."

She was mad at me from earlier; I knew that was contributing to her stubbornness. But I *had* to get her out of here. "We could get arrested!" I said, hoping that would bait her.

She didn't take it.

"Dani, please! Let's just go!"

She flipped me the bird and disappeared back into the dining room to be with Tyler. I had two choices: leave and let her find a way home, knowing she could possibly be tricked into taking drugs or worse; or stay and try to endure this cesspool until she would agree to leave with me. In that moment, I hated her. "You're such an idiot!" I screamed, only to see several people fall silent and turn to look at me. Another round of cheering ensued at the beer pong table and everything went back to normal.

I couldn't leave her here. But when this party was over, she was dead meat.

Three

I LEANED AGAINST the wall in the corner of the dining area, doing my best to shrink out of sight so that I wouldn't be bothered while I kept an eye on Danika. None of our friends were here—none except for a few that I had only talked about the weather with. I couldn't ask anyone to help me shove her into my car kicking and screaming. I briefly wondered why Tyler had invited two of the most straight-laced girls from Ocean View, but then I saw him watching me from across the room. Something in the way his eyes smoldered made me shrink even further, and I hugged my arms tightly around my waist as I diverted my attention elsewhere.

Danika shrieked. "Hands off, jerk!"

My eyes darted to and fro until I saw her marching out of the room. I squeezed between two guys with vodka bottles in their hands and followed her, weaving through the chaos until I saw her jog up the stairs. "Dani, wait!" I called. But of course she didn't.

"Leave me alone, May!" she spat, veering to the left and into a bedroom to lock herself inside.

I pounded on the door, but I could barely hear her over the noise from downstairs. "We need to get out of here. Come on! Let's just go home!"

No answer. Exhaling loudly, I placed my back against the door and closed my eyes. This was a nightmare. I couldn't believe I had let her talk me into this. More than that, I couldn't believe she was acting this way. "You're acting like a child!" I shouted through the door. "You're such a spoiled brat! When are you going to think about someone other than yourself, Danika?"

"O'Hara, are you alright?" Tyler asked, landing on the top step. "I saw you guys run out of there."

He didn't seem as drunk anymore, but his pupils were still wide as saucers. "I'm just trying to get her out so we can leave."

"Ah, don't be ridiculous," he grinned around the words, stepping closer to me to hold out his hand. "Let's just go back downstairs and play some *Sorry*. No drinking. Scout's honor."

"Go to hell."

I turned away from him and went into the next bedroom I could find, but there were bodies moving around under the floral duvet. Disgusted, I kept walking until I found an empty room. I closed myself inside and welcomed a moment alone, catching my breath as my ears hummed from the lack of noise. The bass still thumped below though, and it was enough to make the pictures on the walls rattle.

I went to one of them because it seemed like it could fall off at any time, fixing it because I had nothing better to do. It was a picture of Tyler as a child, and he was kneeling next to a baseball bat, dressed in a red uniform.

This was Tyler's room.

I groaned, sinking down to the hardwood floor beside his bed. I placed my palms on the cold surface below me and relished the temperature. This whole place was like a furnace: a smelly, rotten, drunken furnace. "What did I get us into?" I mumbled, pushing my hands fist-deep into my hair to grab it by the roots.

The door opened and in stepped Tyler. "Enjoying my room?" he smirked, strolling towards me. The open doorway let in more noise and that panicked feeling started to overwhelm me once more.

"Did Danika come out?" I asked sharply.

"Nope." He sat down beside me. "Honestly, it's for the best. Roland Peterson was groping all over her."

I hadn't seen the altercation, but it didn't surprise me when I heard his name. The guy was known for his womanizing tendencies, and he was only one of many. If only the school board knew the types of shenanigans its students frequently partook in. Each member would have had a coronary. Or maybe they did know, and they just didn't care.

I started to get up, but Tyler put his hand on my shoulder. "Just hang out! What are you going to do, go back downstairs and be miserable? At least it's quieter up here."

"It would be quieter if you left."

A grin spread across his face and he folded his arms over his bent knees. "I like you, May. You don't pull any punches. It's refreshing. And this is my room, you know."

I glared at him. "There's no point in being fake. So here's some honesty, Tyler: you're an asshole. Your party? It *sucks*. I would rather eat the crap of a worm-infested rhinoceros than endure another five minutes in this hellhole." My nostrils flared after my rant.

Tyler clapped his hands, applauding me slowly, yet emphatically. "Well said! And you're not wrong. I *am* an asshole."

"An enormous one."

We looked at each other for a long moment as a smirk tugged at both of our lips. Try as I might, I couldn't help it. This whole situation was just *so* absurd. And Tyler may have been an asshole, but at least he wasn't trying to seduce me like he did with so many other girls.

"So what's your favorite color?" he asked.

"What?" I scowled, confused.

"What's your favorite color?" he asked again.

I shook my head. "No, I heard you. It's just a weird question."

"How is it weird? It's a normal question: the kind of question you ask someone when you're trying to get to know them."

I rolled my eyes and crossed my legs in front of me. "I don't care to get to know you, but it's blue."

"Blue." He nodded. "Blue's a good color."

I smiled sarcastically and glanced around the room at his baseball trophy collection, still listening for Danika to come out of the room a few doors down. My fists were aching to strangle her.

"And what's your favorite color, Tyler?" he said theatrically. "Thanks for asking, May! My favorite color is red."

"You're ridiculous," I sighed.

"A little stoned, perhaps. But at least I'm entertaining you."

"I don't need your entertainment. I need this night to be over with."

"Sorry my party is so disappointing." He laced his fingers behind his head and rested back against the mattress. "What's your favorite subject in school?"

I blinked slowly, trying not to grind my teeth hard enough to make them break. "Science."

He didn't say anything in response so I reluctantly peeked at his side profile and inhaled a deep sigh. "And yours?"

"English, I think." His tone had turned serious, and he avoided looking at me. "I love poetry."

I eyed him skeptically. "You like poetry?"

"*Love*," he corrected. Then he went on to quote Shakespeare: "*Ignorance is the curse of God; knowledge is the wing wherewith we fly to heaven.*"

"Impressive," I said, surprised that I meant it. "So why poetry? You don't seem like the creative type."

"I don't know, really. It's just always sort of been my escape from reality."

"Your reality can't be that bad," I said, unconvinced.

He looked at me, hazel eyes sad and serious, though still dilated beyond belief. "If only you knew."

The weight of his stare forced me to look away, but I still felt it burning into the side of my face. "Sorry to hear that."

He shrugged and rested his head against the mattress, looking up at the ceiling. "It's fine. If you think I'm a jerk, you should meet my dad. He blames it on his seizures. Says he has a short fuse. And my mom defends him, but you know? She's just as bad as he is. Sometimes I feel like I haven't made a single choice for myself my entire life."

"I know that feeling, in a way." I looked at him, feeling a little bit of the tension between us breaking away. "But at some point you have to make your own choices and accept the fact that your parents might be disappointed in you."

"See, I get that. I do. But it's not that easy, O'Hara. I have the worst luck; always have. Some people wing it and their life goes according to plan. And it would be my luck that I'd stand up to my dad and then he'd die or something. Choke on his own vomit." He almost sounded like he wanted that to happen.

I didn't know what to say, but I tried to come up with something remotely adequate. "My mom is convinced I'm a lost cause. I don't think she's ever really tried to be a parent. She's exerted all of her efforts onto my sister because she knows I'm too much of a pain in the ass to worry about."

"At least you're on the other end of the spectrum," he smirked. "It's other stuff too. But you don't want to hear the boring details of my sob story."

"I don't mind," I sighed. "It's better than being downstairs in that swarm of filth."

He laughed, examining me. "I'm just glad you showed up."

It wasn't so bad anymore, I had to admit. Tolerable, at least. I nodded awkwardly and hugged my knees to my chest.

He was still smiling, but his gaze relented, and he relaxed against the bed. "Are you a bird or a fish?"

"A what?"

"A bird or a fish," he said, looking at me again while he emphasized each word. "You know, do you swim on the ocean floor with the swarms of those who understand you? Or are you a bird, who flies where you want, when you want, taking control and soaring with independence? There's nothing wrong with either. I'm a fish, myself."

"Huh," I said, tilting my head to the side. "I'd have to say I'm a bird then."

He nodded. "I like being a part of the crowd. In every crowd, there's a hierarchy. Just because you're swimming as part of the crowd, it doesn't mean you don't stand out on your own. But you seem like the type that would take the world by storm and do it mostly on your own."

"What makes you think that?"

The noise from the party downstairs swelled obnoxiously and Tyler stood up. After closing the door, he returned to his spot. "I've seen you at school. Sure, you have your close friends, but you generally don't care about what anyone thinks of you."

"Yes. I think you're right."

He looked at me for a long moment. "You know, you have really pretty eyes."

That uncomfortable feeling surged through me again. "Thank you. So do you."

It happened so quickly that I didn't have time to react. He leaned forward and kissed me. I gasped, breaking away from him. "Tyler," I began, watching his dilated eyes as they examined every part of my face. I scooted an inch or so away. "I don't feel that way about you."

He looked down at his lap, exhaling an embarrassed laugh. When he looked at me again, he was struggling, almost as if he didn't know how to look at me, or what to say.

"Are you okay?" I asked, glancing at the door. It was so far away.

"You know, I'm really not so bad." He brushed the backs of his fingers down my bare arm, eliciting goose bumps which, judging by the grin that lit his face, he assumed were from pleasure.

My heart lunged into a furious tempo. I began to stand up, not even feeling my body move until he grabbed my wrist and pulled me back down onto the floor. "Don't leave," he pleaded. "Come on, May. Just stay."

I looked down at his grip on my wrist, hearing my pulse in my ears. "Please let go."

He looked down at my wrist as well, his eyes narrowing. He almost released me, but then his grip tightened. "No. I'm sick of this."

I swallowed. "What are you sick of?" I was trying to think of ways to keep him calm when everything inside of me screamed to fight free from his grasp.

"Everything," he snapped, jerking me towards him so that our faces were inches apart. "I'm tired of trying to be what I'm not. I'm not nice, May. I'm not what everyone thinks I am."

I was trembling. This situation was quickly escalating and I needed to figure out a way to stop it before it went any further. Tyler was all over the place; unpredictable. It was like he had two voices fighting in his head. "I think you're nice," I said carefully. "I like you, Tyler. I do. It's just that . . . I don't want to get involved with anyone right now."

He scowled. "Do you think I want to get *involved* with you?"

I inhaled unsteadily, trying to keep him from seeing the fear in my eyes. Everything inside of me was coming to a standstill, even my ability to think. I was losing track of how to respond to this. What was I supposed to say? Was I supposed talk him down? Was I supposed to run? "You're so well liked by everyone. You know that, right?"

"I don't care about that. Haven't you ever wanted to break the rules? You are a *bird*, after all."

"Yes," I nodded eagerly. "I want to break the rules. What rule are you wanting to break?"

His grip loosened fractionally, but his body was still rigid.

"What do you want?" I asked again, hoping I could get through to him.

"I want you," he breathed, the alcohol on his breath washing over me.

I shuddered, breathing slowly and deliberately so that I wouldn't hyperventilate. "Please, just let me go. This isn't you."

My words made him snap. He slammed his mouth against mine so hard that my lip split on my teeth. I tried to wrench myself away, but he was too strong. In a mere second, he had me pinned down on the floor, his legs braced over mine to keep me from kicking him. "Stop moving," he growled, slapping my face. He looked at his hand in awe of what he'd just done.

My cheek burned. I started to scream, but he clamped his hand over my mouth. Time stopped. Even though I fought, and even though I begged, he forcefully dragged me onto his bed and shoved my dress up. His shaking hands fumbled with my underwear, tearing them like frail paper. With one hand he held my mouth closed, and with the other he ripped a condom wrapper with his teeth. A few seconds later, pain shot through me like a port directly into my veins. I sobbed against my bent arm, staying still because I had no other choice.

When it was over, he roughly pulled my dress back into place and fixed his clothing. He paced the floor for a long time, squeezing the spot between his eyes. "What did I do?" he said beneath his heaving breath.

I started to slip off of the bed to escape, but he faced me at that moment. His eyes were wild and confused. My heart stuttered and froze.

And then he disappeared without another word to justify what he had just done.

Four

Now

THE WIND WHIPS my face as I sit on a blanket, peering out over the ocean from my place on Agate Beach. The sun is setting and its rays ripple across the waves as they beat the sandy shore. Elijah, my husband, walks across the sand with our daughter swaddled securely against his chest. His pants are rolled up to his knees to keep them dry. He stops and looks out toward the horizon, bending down to pick up something that just washed up at his feet.

He turns around and grins at me, then gently takes one of Addison's tiny hands, making her wave. I wave back and smile, patting the spot next to me.

He brings her to me, carefully lowering her into my arms, and then takes his place beside me. I feel him rub my back as he kisses my shoulder. "She likes the waves," he says quietly.

I lay her down in my lap, resting her head near my knees as she wraps both hands around my thumbs. She coos softly, squeezing my fingers as she grins. I rest my head on Elijah's shoulder and exhale contentedly. Today is the anniversary of one of the worst days of my life. He knows it too. That's why he brought us here; he wants me to have peace.

I have everything I need.

Then

"DANIKA!" I CRIED hoarsely as my fists pounded the door that was still locked.

"I'm right here."

I turned around and saw her watching me. "Where were you?"

"I was trying to find you," she explained. "Are you alright?"

I grabbed her wrist and pulled her down the stairs with me. "We have to go. Now."

"Alright, I'm coming! What's wrong with you?" she begged. I continued to tow her out the front door.

"Nothing." My eyes burned like they were on fire. If I could just make it to the car; make it to her house; make it *home* without feeling the full weight of what had just happened, I would be able to manage this. *Prioritize, May.* I told myself these things to make it easier to put them on the back burner, but the residual searing pain was a constant reminder that I was only fooling myself. "I just don't feel good. Someone gave me a weird drink."

"Well, at least *one* of us got to have fun," she said tersely, climbing into the passenger seat of my car. "But are you sober enough to drive?"

I got in on my side and put the keys into the ignition with a trembling hand, thankful the darkness was enough to shroud my face. I didn't want to talk about what really happened. I never wanted anyone to know. The humiliation I felt was more prevalent than any other feeling I could fathom, enough so that I wanted to hide in a dark room and never emerge. "I'm fine," I promised.

"That guy Dane is pretty hot. At least *he* wasn't too preoccupied with you to look my way."

My throat clenched as I floored it through a yellow light, seeing it turn red before I even crossed the line. I wanted to pull the car over and scream at her; tear her apart for being so selfish; make her feel like the worst woman alive, because in that moment, I believed she was.

"Are you going to throw up?" she asked suspiciously, leaning closer to her window.

My car squealed to a stop outside of her house. "I'll see you on Monday." My hands fisted the steering wheel so hard my knuckles ached.

"May?"
"Get out."
She stared at me. "What did I—"
"Get. Out."
And she did.

* * *

I STEPPED INTO my house with a slight limp, hardly remembering the drive home. My lip felt swollen. Everything hurt. I walked numbly up the stairs and went into my bathroom to shower; I had never felt more dirty in my entire life.

Removing my dress was painful. I tried not to look in the mirror, but I caught a glimpse and couldn't look away. My lip wasn't as bad as it felt; probably not even noticeable to anyone else. There were no visible bruises on my body. Looking at myself, it was easy to imagine that I had dreamed it; that I would wake up tomorrow and breathe a sigh of relief that it hadn't been real. But then a memory of Tyler tearing his way into me while I stared helplessly at the ceiling made me rush to the toilet, heaving for what felt like an eternity. I sobbed, clutching the icy porcelain.

I finally sank down with my back against the cabinets until I could hug my knees to my chest. That was when the shaking began, stealing control of my entire body. And that was when I replayed everything that had happened, trying to make sense of it; trying to understand what I had done wrong to instigate him.

What did I do? His frantic voice returned to mind.

He had hit me; I hadn't asked for that. He had taken control. Yet his response when it was over contradicted his actions, and somehow I knew I had misunderstood.

I was so confused. My cheek still throbbed where he had slapped me. Steam from the shower clouded around me in a suffocating haze as I gripped the bathroom rug beneath me. It was the only thing that made me feel somewhat stable. I sat there until sweat began to roll off my face. I tried to understand. I tried to understand what I had done to ask for this.

But no matter how much I reasoned with each passing thought, and no matter how many times I tried to recall what I had done to instigate him, the reality of what had happened was finally crashing down over me. There was only one explanation: one that I never in a million years thought would be something I would have to experience firsthand.

I had been raped.

And I had no idea what to do.

Five

I WAS UP AT LEAST three times to vomit that night. Each time I began to drift to sleep, I felt it all over again; not the nausea, but Tyler's hands. I saw his face. I smelled the alcohol on his breath. I could make myself think about other things until that moment right before the dreams took over, at which I was being held down all over again. Each time sent me running to the bathroom. Each time, I had to resist the urge to sob, because I didn't want my dad to hear my cries and find out what had happened to me.

I had been asleep for less than an hour when my alarm blared, thrusting me out of a dream I'd finally managed to put myself into—one where I felt safe. Warm. So when my eyes snapped open to the cold reality I was living, it was as if I had ventured into a snowy wasteland, naked and alone.

I reached for my alarm and turned it off. As I sat up, I found Grace standing in my doorway with a cup of water. She approached me. "I heard you getting sick all night. You need to stay hydrated."

I took the glass from her. "Thank you," I croaked. I brought it to my lips and sipped, lying back to rest on my pillows. "Shouldn't you be getting ready for your riding lesson?" I forced a smile, noticing she was still in her nightgown.

"I am. I just wanted to make sure you were okay. Dad's downstairs, if you want me to get him."

"No," I shook my head. "It's okay. I'm okay. Must have just eaten something bad."

She frowned and nodded, then turned toward the door. "We'll be back later."

I took a few drinks of water before I put the glass aside and slowly climbed out of bed. I gasped sharply when I took my first step toward the bathroom, the dull ache even more painful than before. When I sat down on the toilet, I found blood in my underwear.

I trembled all over again and barely felt tears begin to fall. For a while I sat there staring at the streak of red, trying to imagine another scenario that could have caused it. Nothing came to mind. I couldn't will this away. This wasn't a nightmare I could wake up from. I had been used and discarded by someone who couldn't even be bothered to ask if I wanted it.

My cries became louder until I reached over and turned on the shower, biting down on my balled fist to stifle it. I noticed my cell phone was still on the counter from the night before, so I reached for it and pulled up Addison's text feed.

Addison: It's so beautiful here, May! You should have come!

I should have. I began typing.

Me: Addison, I need you.

The tears were fresh again, this time falling soundlessly. I stared at my phone as I tried to recall what time it was in Italy. Five in the afternoon? Six? Surely she was awake.

My phone started ringing and displayed a picture of Addison making a silly face. I answered it and pressed it against my wet cheek. "I don't want to talk about it. I just needed to hear your voice."

"May," she said, distraught as though she could feel my pain without even knowing the cause. "Please talk to me. You're scaring me."

I wept for a moment, trying to keep it quiet but failing. I couldn't say it out loud. I didn't know if I would ever muster the courage to do so. So instead I told her half of the truth: the half that didn't hurt nearly as badly as the other. "I lost my virginity last night."

She was quiet for a couple beats, and then she asked me the question that only she would ask: "How is your heart?"

I tried to swallow, but I couldn't. "It hurts. I wish I could take it back."

"It'll be okay, May. It's okay to hurt. It's okay to make mistakes. Don't let anyone tell you that you don't have a right to be upset about this, because you do. This is *your* moment to feel whatever you need to feel."

"I feel so stupid," I groaned. "I'm so stupid!"

"You are *not* stupid. Someday I'll ask you who he was and what happened, but not today." She knew me very well and I loved her even more for that. "But do something for me, alright?"

"Anything," I whispered.

"Do something soon that makes last night seem like a distant memory, even if only for a while. The rest of the time, feel everything. Let it process. You have every reason and right to feel it all. Take as long as you need. And remember that whoever this guy is might have been your first, but what counts is the person that'll be your forever. He doesn't own you. He may have your virginity but he doesn't get to own your heart, not unless you want him to. Don't let this degrade you."

I smiled sadly. "Thanks, Addi."

"Love you."

"You too."

The call ended and I laid my phone back on the counter. After cleaning up and sneaking through the house to toss my soiled clothing into the wash, I went back to my bed and buried myself under the covers.

* * *

I DIDN'T EMERGE for three days. My parents bought the lie that I had a horrible stomach bug because I had the vomiting to prove it, so other than keeping me hydrated and bringing me crackers, my illness wasn't questioned. The thing was that I didn't feel sick; it would just overcome me the moment I started to fall asleep.

I didn't cry. I didn't think. I just *was*. It was as if my brain were detached from my body until I couldn't stay awake any longer. As the days passed, I only grew worse. My stomach was sinking in on itself and in the times I couldn't avoid going to the bathroom anymore, I could see the sleep deprivation on my face.

And I could finally see the bruises: deep, blotchy, black and blue.

Having a doctor for a father was both a blessing and a curse. In this situation, it was a blessing. Most parents would have rushed me to the ER by now. My dad wasn't so quick to panic. "If she stops eating or if she's still throwing up tomorrow, I'll take her in," he had told my mom, who had only checked on me once. She was out of town again so the five minutes she spent at my bedside were brief and I barely remembered them. But the less supervision I had, the less questions would be asked. Mom always knew when I was lying anyway.

I never checked my phone. Nobody came to visit. Nobody *would* have other than Danika and Addison anyway, and Addison was still out of the country. My teachers informed my dad that my homework was piling up, and he continued to tell them that I was still too ill to return. But I could tell he was beginning to question whether or not my absence from school was still warranted because I had been able to keep food down for twenty-four hours.

On day four, I knew I had to get out of bed. I spent an hour under water that was hot enough to make my skin raw. I washed away the grime and sweat that had accumulated on my body, but it did nothing to thaw out my mind. I still felt numb; detached. And I knew I didn't have any more lies left in me. If I allowed myself to actually *talk* to my dad, a plea would tumble forth that I wouldn't be able to contain. I wanted to be taken out of my school and placed into the public school system. I didn't want to have to face Tyler.

But Dad would ask why, and I knew I didn't have it in me to give him something convincing. So I said nothing at all.

Six

I STOOD BY MY CAR, looking across the parking lot at the entrance to my school. The doors seemed like a death trap as students made their way inside. I had covered my bruises with my student-assigned uniform jacket and a pair of black leggings, and reasoned with myself in the mirror before I left my house, but I still felt ill-prepared. I wasn't ready to see him. "Keep your head up, May," I told myself, taking the first step across the asphalt.

Maybe if he didn't see that I was wounded inside and out, he wouldn't approach me. Maybe he would forget about it if he hadn't already. Maybe he had been too high to remember anyway.

My eyes darted in every direction when I stepped inside the entrance. I wanted to avoid eye contact with *anyone*, but I couldn't seem to control where I looked. It was a sea of uniformly dressed teenagers who all looked the same in my mind's eye. Male and female. That was all they were, because their faces didn't matter.

And then I saw him. He stood at his locker, retrieving what he would need for class. I stopped walking. He looked my way.

For a moment I thought he was going to say something, but instead his jaw clamped shut and he slammed his locker so hard it made me jump. He turned away without another look and went into the very classroom that I would be forced to join in a matter of moments.

He was angry, and I could feel that anger reaching into every cell of my body as though it were directed at me; as though he believed that *I* caused him to do the unthinkable. Or perhaps he was only angry at himself, and seeing me was a reminder of that. Either way, when Tyler Jenkins left me standing there, one thought resounded that made me angry at *myself*: I wanted answers.

I hardly realized I was looking at Danika until her head tilted and she released a sigh. I shook my head to escape my trance. "Hey," I managed.

"Are you feeling better?"

"All better." I hoped she bought it.

She closed her eyes as though she was trying to arrange what she was about to say. When she opened them again, they were full of tears. "I'm sorry, May. You were right. I *was* being selfish." She watched me for a moment but I could feel my expression staying the same, contorted by what I had witnessed before at Tyler's locker. "I just can't stand what's going on between us. I feel like you hate me. I mean, yeah . . . I made you miserable the other night. And I was rude. But that kind of thing wouldn't have made you react like this before, so I know there's more to it. There's more to it, right?"

I felt my face adopt a new look, but I couldn't tell what it was. "I just need a break, Danika. I know you want an explanation but . . . I just have a lot going on. I need to think about my own life." It was more than I had said in days, and it felt strange; as if the words didn't belong in my mouth.

Was it even true? Did I want to think about myself?

I had gone to that party for her. I had stayed for her. My virginity had been stolen in the most unthinkable way possible, all for *her*. How could I tell her that even being near her was like sandpaper on my wounds? It didn't matter though, because she hugged her books tighter to her body and lifted her chin stiffly, not even dignifying me with an answer before turning on her heel and entering the classroom.

That *was* my answer. And I was relieved because I could hardly stand the sight of her.

* * *

I SANK INTO MY SEAT as inconspicuously as possible while the other students in English class prepared for our first lesson of the day. I kept my eyes on my book as I counted down the seconds until it would begin. A few papers were set before me and I slowly lifted my eyes to the giver of them.

"Good morning, class," Mr. Cannon said, stroking his long, gray beard as he looked up from my desk. He cleared his throat loudly. "By Friday, I want each of you to write a poem in the style of either a stanza or a sonnet. I want that poem to be full of imagery. And on that note, the first person to accurately quote *I Know Why the Caged Bird Sings* by Maya Angelou this morning will get an automatic A on that assignment. Though, to be perfectly honest, I don't expect any of you to know it by heart. Who wants to give it a go?" he asked, sitting down in his chair.

I knew this poem by heart. I had first heard it as a little girl, when my aunt Elizabeth read it from her poetry book while we sat together on her front porch one summer. I found it so beautiful that I memorized it, and I'd never forgotten it. The bird in the poem was caged, locked away only to watch another bird fly free and without a care in the distance. So the caged bird could only sing, wishing for that freedom too. I waited for someone to volunteer, because I could feel my heart thrashing at the prospect of standing up with Tyler's eyes on my back.

"I'll do it," Tyler said behind me.

I heard him stand up and then he began. His voice was confident but heavy, as if he were pondering each word while he said it. My palms grew clammy, leaving handprints on my desk. I wiped them on my skirt and forced myself to breathe. But I could feel him. I could feel him watching me.

I knew how that bird felt. I knew exactly.

"Are you a bird or a fish?" Tyler's question from the other day came to mind.

What a cruel question to ask someone before trying to break their wings.

* * *

I WASN'T SURE how I made it through the school day alive. I only had two classes that Tyler didn't share, and those were the only two I had been able to remotely concentrate in. My grades were bound to suffer, so I knew I had to find a way to focus the rest of the week.

After making Grace dinner, I sat at the kitchen island to recover. My eyes felt as if they were coated with sand. My muscles and bones ached like I had the flu. I just wanted to sleep, but I had homework. Lots and lots of homework.

I was just opening my poetry book when my phone dinged with a text from Danika. I opened it, feeling the wind getting knocked out of me.

Danika: Day. Made. I had sex with Tyler after school! I made the walk of shame out of his house. Lol.

I laid the phone down and rested my forehead on my palm, focusing on my breathing. Another text.

Danika: That was for Addison. Sorry . . .

The front door opened and closed, and I quickly recomposed myself, pretending to be reading from my book. But my chest was quaking with each heartbeat. My vision grew fuzzy and my hearing felt skewed.

"How was school? And your weekend?" Mom asked, entering the kitchen to set her purse and briefcase down on the counter. She opened the fridge, tapping her leather pump-clad foot.

I didn't even realize how much I was dreading facing her again until that moment. Dad was clueless except for when he was working on somebody's brain. Aside from spelling it out for him, he hardly noticed anything was amiss. Mom, on the other hand? She was paid to analyze people and to pick up on all their dirty secrets. She always knew when I was lying. *Always.*

I lifted my head to look at her. "Fine," I lied as smoothly as I could.

"Good," she nodded, leaning against the counter with a bottle of water in hand. Her dress suit accentuated her hourglass body. She regarded me with scrutinizing green eyes. "What did you learn?"

I recognized this trick. She knew how to tell when I was lying, and I knew how to tell when she was prodding me with pseudo kindness to get me to reveal that I was lying. I decided to stick as close to the truth as possible. "I had trouble concentrating. I was sick this weekend, and I'm still feeling under the weather."

She frowned. "Did your dad examine you?"

"No," I answered, closing my book. "I'm okay. Just worn out."

"Alright," she said, pursing her lips. "Well, finish your homework and go to bed. I'll help Grace with her schoolwork tonight."

"Are you sure?" I asked, trying not to sound too skeptical. Mom rarely let me off the hook this easily.

"I'm sure. You look pale. I'll be in my office. When you're feeling better, I want you to start working on your college applications."

College: the word my world had revolved around for months and months, yet the same word I hadn't even thought about since Friday. "I will," I promised, hoping it would be a suitable distraction. I needed to start focusing on my future rather than the past.

Mom left the kitchen and I felt my labored breathing return. I propped up my forehead in my sweaty palm and tried to get myself under control. Another text, but this one was from Addison.

Addison: I'm hoooome!

I nearly crumbled in relief.

Me: Welcome back. Tired?

Addison: Very. But you should come over.

I didn't have to think twice. I grabbed my book bag and poked my head into Mom's office. "I'm going to Addison's to finish my homework. She just made it back."

"Aren't you ill?" she frowned, eyeing me.

"Just tired," I reiterated. "But not too tired to hear about her trip."

"Alright. Just an hour or two. You need to be rested. It's only Tuesday."

"Promise. Thanks, Mom."

And I felt a genuine sense that I would be okay if I could just step through Addison's door and see her smiling face.

* * *

"FINALLY!" MY FRIEND EXCLAIMED, opening the door before my knock. She practically leapt into my arms. She smelled like airplane, clad in yoga pants and a hoodie, with her brunette hair in the messiest bun I had ever seen, but she was still beautiful. I squeezed her with all I had and when I let her go, she dragged me into her house by my hand.

"Hello, May!" her mother grinned. "It's good to see you."

"Hello, Mrs. Flood. Thank you for letting me come over."

She stirred a steaming pot with a wooden spoon and winked my way. "You know you're always welcome here, darlin'."

I had always felt more welcome at the Floods' than in my own home. I smiled at her and followed Addison to her bedroom, and she closed the door. We both made a beeline for her enormous beanbag chair. We plopped onto it, stretching out our limbs. Addison was laughing; I was trying to.

"So," she began, rolling onto her side to face me. Her brown eyes were tired but they were still bright. "How are you?"

"I should be asking you that. I want to hear all about your trip."

"Well," she smiled dreamily, propping her head up on her bent arm. "It was magical. Everything about it was like a dream. The scenery, the history . . . the people and food," she grinned and then laughed. "Especially the food."

"Mmm. Genuine Italian food," I said, forcing a small smile. "What else?"

"Well, the boys weren't bad to look at either," she smirked. "But I was more focused on the culture. Learned a *lot*."

"Like what?"

"Well, the way people interact is *so* different. How you dress and present yourself is vital. I never thought of that! When I first got there, I felt like I was being sized up. And people are late to everything," she laughed. "But it's not a big deal to them. Lots of enthusiasm all around."

She looked at the ceiling and sighed longingly. "I could live there. I really could. When I first went to the Pantheon, I was instantly overwhelmed with tears. Same with the Colosseum, but for different reasons." She looked at me again. "You *have* to go with me next time, May. It was absolutely life changing."

I knew people went to Italy all the time, but for Addison, it wasn't just something to mark off her bucket list. It was her history. And though it wasn't mine, I someday wanted to share it with her. "I promise I'll go next time, come hell or high water."

"Good," she smiled. "There's so much more, but I'll tell you later." Her smile faded and her eyes grew serious. "Talk to me about *you*. How are you after Friday?"

I had thought seeing Addison would be enough for me to finally admit to somebody what had actually happened. But the longer I looked at her, the more I realized I wasn't ready. "It's still hard," was all I could say.

She was quiet for a moment, thinking. Addison never spoke before she thought, and I appreciated it because I knew that whatever she said was exactly how she intended it. Sometimes the truth she spoke was tough to hear; other times it spoke right to my soul. "He wasn't the one," she said.

My eyes watered. Of course he wasn't "the one," but that wasn't what she meant. She meant it so much deeper than that. It wasn't as though she was stating a fact I didn't already know, but instead reflecting a thought I didn't even know I had been harboring. Cruelty aside, pain and confusion aside, I had been robbed of something I could never get back: my innocence. I had never even kissed a boy before. I had never seen a man naked. My view of sex would forever be skewed, and that was what I was robbed of. It wasn't even about losing my virginity. It was about losing the part of me that would ever be able to imagine sex as beautiful.

"He wasn't the one," I repeated.

"Do you blame yourself?"

I could almost hear my own heartbeat. I didn't want to talk about this. I had been counting on Addison's return so she could help me make sense of it, but now that she was here, I was frozen. How was it that I couldn't even admit the truth to my kindred spirit? I felt a rope around my neck, choking the words out of me. I felt them seizing on the tip of my tongue. *I was raped. I need to tell you that I was raped.* "How can I not?" I offered instead. "I could have prevented it somehow."

She frowned, perplexed by my words. And I instantly began to backtrack because I could see she was beginning to recognize there was more to this than I was letting on. "I mean, I could have said no, you know? Or left the room so we weren't alone."

"This was at the party you and Danika went to?"

I rubbed my lips together. *How did she know about that?* "Yes. Danika went off on her own and I was alone with a guy. Stupid," I sighed heavily, frustrated.

She nodded. "She texted me that night and said you guys were fighting after the party. She sounded pretty upset, but she didn't explain."

"Please don't tell her about this." I could hear a quiver in my voice and I desperately tried to steady it. "I don't want her to know about it."

"I won't. Promise."

I knew she wasn't saying something. I knew by the way her coffee-colored eyes glassed over that she knew there was more to the story—more than I was willing to admit. She didn't pry. Instead she scooted forward on the beanbag chair and hugged me tightly. My head came to rest under her chin and I could feel the rapid pulse of her heart thumping against my ear. It was proof she was containing something painful; something that filled her with dread. It was the way a heart beats inside a person when they have something to ask, but they're afraid of the answer. So I changed the subject because deep down, I knew what that question would be.

"We have a substitute English teacher for a couple months. I heard Mr. Pierce had heart surgery and there were some complications."

"That's awful." I felt her shake her head. "I hope he's going to be okay. What is the new teacher like?"

"Strict and cocky," I sighed. "He looks like Gandalf from *The Lord of the Rings*. He's having us write poems this week. Any style we want."

"I *love* sonnets. I think that's what I'll do."

"Awesome."

I closed my eyes. Addison's heart still jogged at the same pace. Something in me wanted to flee before the dam broke and she asked me the question I knew was churning within her. "I'm going to go so you can get some sleep. You must be exhausted." I sat up and made my way to my feet. When I looked down at her, I saw her watching me; examining me; peeling away my layers to see the truth. And everything inside of me wanted to escape. "I'll see you at school tomorrow, Addi. I'm glad you're back."

Her eyes softened fractionally. "Night, May. See you tomorrow."

I barely made it to my car before crumbling against my steering wheel, my breath stolen by painful sobs.

Seven

I GAVE SCHOOL an honest try. I really did. But that night, the same dreams returned and though I wasn't ill from them, they were taking over me in a new way:

I couldn't stop crying. I couldn't stop groaning into my pillow from the pain of my wounds and the misery in my heart. I wanted to escape; I wanted everything to disappear. I never wanted anyone to see the truth, and the more time that passed, the more transparent I felt I was becoming. I knew I should tell someone. Maybe unloading this burden would have made it easier to process. I heard before that rape victims often felt ashamed, but I never comprehended how that could be possible until it happened to me.

I was so, *so* ashamed. And every day, I was lost in a mental prison that made me both numb and hypersensitive to everything I encountered. It took every ounce of my energy to even get out of bed to use the restroom, and showering drained me completely, but I wanted to do it all the time. Twice a day, if not more. Wake up, survive, sleep, repeat.

When Friday came, Mom finally insisted that I be examined at the hospital. "She's not getting better," she told one of my dad's colleagues while I sat in a cotton gown on the cushioned table. "She was throwing up earlier this week, but we assumed she had a virus. She's been really puny since."

"Sometimes the body is still fighting off the virus even after the worst symptoms resolve themselves," Dr. Fletcher explained, inserting a thermometer into my ear. "Any stomach cramps, diarrhea, chills, body aches . . . ?"

"No," I murmured. How could I explain that a virus had nothing to do with it? How could I get out of this and leave them satisfied that it was nothing of concern?

"Mrs. O'Hara, may I speak to your daughter privately for a moment?"

Her eyes widened. "She's seventeen. You can't be serious. I have a right to know what's going on here!"

He pulled her aside and spoke quietly. I couldn't hear him, but I could see Mom's face.

"Of course it's nothing else!" she hissed. "She's just sick."

"Mrs. O'Hara, please . . ." his voice trailed off.

She looked at me and tilted her chin up indignantly as she left the room. He closed the door behind her and then faced me, his eyes softening. "May, I have a question." He approached and then sat down on his stool before me. "Are you really feeling sick?"

I shook my head, confused. Did he not believe me? Did I need to come up with another lie? "Of course. Maybe it's something else . . ."

"I believe it is," he nodded. "Are you feeling depressed? Anxious? Are you having issues at school?"

I gulped, feeling as though I was underneath an enormous microscope. The only difference was that his face wasn't distorted through the glass; instead he was caring and attentive. I felt my eyes flood. My lips trembled. I cursed myself for it. "People are just cruel," I stammered. "At school, I mean. I don't want to go back."

He frowned sadly. I had known Dr. Fletcher since I was born, which was part of the reason I avoided this for an entire week. He had always been able to see the deeper issue, but it had never been something *this* deep before. "Are you being bullied?"

I almost scoffed. *Bullied*? What was this, elementary school? "Not really. It's hard to explain. I don't want to explain it. I just want out."

"May," he said, imploring me to focus on his warm, brown eyes. "Did something happen in particular?"

Anyone else would have crumbled. Hell, even *I* would have crumbled if I wasn't so angry. I felt my blood beginning to simmer and soon it would boil over. I knew better than to confide in him. He was legally obligated to report the truth if I were to offer it. "Nothing happened. I just don't want to be there anymore."

He sighed, relenting as he scribbled something on his clipboard. "Do you feel anxious around big groups of people? Do you think that might be it?"

Anxious. Social Anxiety. Grace had issues with that, so it wouldn't be hard to assume I could have it too. Hope filled me at the thought that perhaps I could finish my studies at home. "Yes, that's it, I think."

"I'm sorry," he said compassionately. "Have you distanced yourself from anything you usually love doing? Any hobbies?"

"I haven't painted in a while . . ." I admitted, not even realizing until then that my passion for it had fallen away. I had no desire to do it anymore. "I do still want to ride my horse though."

"Horses are great therapy for a lot of different things. You have a relationship with your horse that is safe and comforting, because he can never judge you for your faults. I completely understand."

I nodded, hanging my head to look at my hands in my lap.

"I'll let your mom know I'm prescribing something for your anxiety. I need you to fill out this questionnaire for me, alright? It'll give me a better idea of the proper treatment to prescribe."

He handed me another clipboard with a form that had a long list of questions. At the top was a rating system. Within that list was a question that caused me to lock up for several minutes after his departure: *Do you feel that you are a guilty person who deserves to be punished*?

Was this all my fault?

I heard Dr. Fletcher speaking to my mom in the hallway outside. "I think she's depressed," he told her. "I'm not sure to what degree yet, but she's taking a test now. I also think she's struggling with social anxiety."

"So what is the plan?" Mom asked after a moment of silence.

"When she's finished with her test, I'll know what direction to take. I recommend she try the medication for a couple weeks before you decide what might be better for her health."

"What do you mean?"

"I mean she might do better in a smaller group setting, or even studying on her own."

I could hear my mother's frustrated sigh, but in that sigh, I also heard acceptance.

Half an hour later, Mom was given a white slip with some scribbles on it and I was told to keep my chin up. The ride to the pharmacy and then to our home was awkward and confining. Mom asked me things like, "When did this start?" and "Why didn't you say something?"

But my answer was simple and I only said it once: "I just wasn't ready to admit I was feeling this way."

Thankfully it satisfied her, but I could sense disappointment. I was her strong one. I was the one who never let anything get me down. I was the one who never needed help with my studies, and certainly never with keeping my path straight. But what she didn't know was that all of that was just a mirror image of her: appearances to keep things tightly knit together. I had always secretly felt out of control. But at least I had always had the open sky to correct my course when the wind became too strong.

Now I didn't know where I belonged.

Now

ELIJAH PULLS ME into his chest, both of us breathless. My body hums with relief; my heart thrashes wildly. I smile as I rest my face in the crook of his neck, feeling his pulse pounding under my hand and against my lips when I kiss him there. "I love you," I whisper, feeling his arms tighten around me.

"I love you," he responds, catching his breath. He turns onto his side so that my head is on his bicep, and he stares at me with eyes the color of a stormy ocean. His hand rests on my cheek as he places a lingering kiss on my lips. "How are you feeling?"

"Spent," I laugh, but I know that's not what he means. The serious look in his eyes affirms that. I lay my hand over his. "I'm alright. I have you and Addison. You both helped me get through this week."

He kisses my forehead, trailing the backs of his fingers down my arm. "As always, anything you need . . . I'm here."

"I know," I smile, glancing to where my red scarf lays on the dresser on the other side of the room. But I can't think of that now. All I want to think about is the man in my arms and the sleeping infant in the next room of this little bed and breakfast as the waves crash outside.

Then

I SQUEEZED THE REMAINING water out of my hair with a towel as I stood naked before my bedroom's floor-length mirror. I examined a few bruises on my legs and one on my shoulder from where Tyler pinned me down with his elbow. They were yellow and purple and seemed to be fading. I touched them lightly and saw in my mind's eye the entire thing from start to finish, thankful that this time I didn't fall apart.

But nightmares followed me to bed that night just like before. Only this time, I didn't wake up from them. They plagued me from the moment I fell asleep until a sound outside jolted me back to life.

I lunged upright in bed, heaving for breath. Sweat trickled down my face and neck. The room was too dark; it was suffocating me. I reached for my lamp but it wouldn't turn on, so I darted across the room to flip on the light. The power was out. The tree outside crashed against my window with a gust of angry wind. I raked air into my lungs, pressing my back against the wall as I sank to my knees. I couldn't even remember what I had dreamt. I only knew what I felt.

My body shook with each sob, my bare legs hugged tightly to my chest. This all just needed to end. I felt like I was losing my sanity more with each passing hour.

"May?" Mom called through my door. "I brought you a lantern."

I got to my feet and reached for the door to open it. She stood on the other side with two lanterns in hand, their light making the space between us glow. I took one of them and cursed my shaking hand.

"Are you alright?" she asked. "It's just a storm."

"I'm fine," I lied. "It just scared me is all."

"It was certainly a rude awakening. Your father and Grace are on the couch downstairs. Do you want to join us?"

Tears unexpectedly flooded my eyes again and I stepped forward, clinging to my mom in a way I hadn't done since I was a child. She stiffly patted my back. "You really were scared, weren't you?" she soothed in the best manner she knew how.

If only you knew. "Yes." I shook as I pulled away. She put her arm around me and guided me downstairs and into the living room where Dad and Grace were sitting together under a blanket.

"There's my other girl," Dad grinned. "Come here, Dewdrop."

Dad's nickname for me always brought back memories of when he would lie with me on the couch to watch cartoons on Saturday mornings when I was little. He only used it rarely now.

I sat down on the other side of him and he put the blanket over my lap. Mom went to the fireplace and turned the dial a bit to help the flames grow. She then sat on the other side of our sectional, using her own blanket to cover herself up.

"Do you girls remember the storm that blew through about five years ago? I was actually concerned for our house with that one," Dad recalled. "I watched the news last night. This one just sounds mean, but it's really not so bad."

"I just hope the roof is still intact when it passes," Mom sighed.

I rested my head on Dad's shoulder and let out a long breath. The flames danced when the wind blasted down the chimney again. Something about this moment was comforting; I couldn't remember the last time our whole family had sat together in the same room for more than thirty minutes at dinnertime, let alone under blankets on the couch. I closed my eyes and listened to the rain.

"Who wants to play *Monopoly?*" Dad suggested.

I opened my eyes in time to see Mom roll hers. *Board games.* I didn't think I could ever think of them the same way again. I lifted my head and looked at Dad. I could see in his eyes he was actually excited about the idea.

"I'll play," I said softly, but not for me. For him.

And until sunrise, that is precisely what we did.

Eight

I WOKE THE NEXT MORNING, realizing that for the first time I actually felt like going to the stable. I found that Dad had already left with Grace, so I took my own car. I welcomed the time alone anyway. At least I didn't feel like crying anymore.

My phone dinged as I was rolling up to a stop light. A text from Danika flashed on the screen.

Danika: Are you still mad at me?

I locked my phone and tossed it into my purse where I wouldn't see it again. When it continued to alert me of incoming messages, I turned up the radio to drown it out. I looked around the green forest canopying the winding road. Facets of sunlight broke through now and then and glistened in the misty air like floating diamonds. But I couldn't even appreciate the beauty of this familiar road like I so often did, because in my mind's eye, I was seeing something else entirely.

I still didn't know what to do. I was scared to tell anybody; not because I feared that Tyler would threaten my life, but because for some strange reason, I still felt like I was at least somewhat at fault. Maybe I didn't fight hard enough. Maybe that wasn't Tyler at all, and the drugs had their way with him. But I recalled the way he looked at me for a fraction of a second when I told him that his life couldn't have been all that bad. For some reason, that look haunted me almost as much as the rest of it.

And would anyone even believe me? Would anyone take the dumb girl from the party's word over his? Tyler had more love from a wider array of people than me. *Everybody* knew his name. He was always praised for his academics and beloved by most groups at our school. Hardly anyone could pick me out in a crowd if asked to.

Time. That was what I needed. I just needed to make sense of this; to put the pieces together.

Was it normal to be this ashamed of myself? Was it normal not to be seething with hatred for him? It wasn't as though we had a friendship prior, or any semblance of one, but for some reason, I didn't hate him for what he did.

Or maybe I just didn't hate him yet.

* * *

GRACE WAS POSTING in the saddle as her horse trotted around the arena with perfect form. I watched her as I parked my car in the designated spot for the stable's boarders, noticing that Dad was standing in the middle and videotaping her on his phone with his own horse's reins in hand. Grace smiled at me when she passed by the rail again. Honestly? I think she only ever smiled when she was on a horse.

I walked around to the other side of my car and opened the door to retrieve my boots, slipping out of my sneakers to put them on. After tucking my jeans inside of them, I made my way into the barn.

The smell soothed me. I went to the rack of halters and picked up the one that said *Cash* across the leather-covered noseband, and slung it over my shoulder as I approached my horse's stall. He was nose-deep in his grain bucket. "Morning," I smirked, lifting the latch on his door. It slid open with ease and I stepped inside. He raised his head and watched me with enormous brown eyes, his jaws still working to chew his mouthful.

His black coat was glossy and clean, aside from a dusting of wood shavings on his back from rolling in his stall. And even though he didn't really need it, I planned on giving him a bath. "Let's go," I said, slipping the halter over his face. I led him into the breezeway, his shoes clip-clopping across the cement as we headed to the wash rack outside. After looping his rope around the metal piping, I went inside to get the necessary supplies.

Shampoo. Conditioner. Coat polisher. Hoof polish. Rubber bands. Brushes. I put all of it into a bucket and ventured back outside, seeing my dad riding toward me.

"Not going to ride?" he asked.

"Not today," I answered, setting the bucket down. Cash was half asleep as he waited for me. "Just wanted to groom him."

"He's already clean," he chuckled. The sun glinted off his glossy boots and spurs; his pristine saddle and bridle. "Come on. Grace would love to ride with you."

"I know, but I would rather just relax this time."

"Alright," he said, shaking his head as he rode past me into the barn.

I watched him disappear from view and exhaled a slow breath while I turned the water on. The hose expanded all the way to the end, stopped by the spray nozzle attached there. I picked it up and turned the dial, squeezing the lever to release a strong mist. I started with Cash's feet and his eyes opened, but he didn't fidget.

"Feel good?" I sighed, working upward toward his legs and then his body. I sprayed over his rump and back, moving up to his neck, saturating his long, wavy mane, and did the same on the other side. A flash of light reflected on a windshield as another car pulled into the lot. I didn't recognize it. A man emerged sporting a baseball cap, faded jeans, and a blue t-shirt. He jogged toward the barn and nodded to me in passing, saying, "Good morning!"

A new boarder, perhaps? He couldn't have been older than twenty-five, but I didn't see his face all that well. "Morning," I acknowledged, even though he was already inside the barn. I laid the hose down and squirted a line of shampoo down Cash's back, all the way from his ears to his tail. Then I picked up a rubber curry and started to lather him in small circles.

The same man emerged on the bare back of a tall, chestnut-colored horse, using only a halter and lead rope. He rode toward me and stopped, observing what I was doing. "My horse has been here for a while, but I haven't been able to come here often," he said. "I'm Alex."

I looked up at him, shielding my eyes from the sun with my dripping forearm. He looked younger than twenty-five. Maybe twenty. His eyes matched his shirt; bright blue, like a tropical ocean. They sparkled warmly. "May," I said quietly. I didn't really feel like talking. "Are you from around here?"

"Portland, actually. I just moved to Newport."

I squinted, but not from the sun. My little hometown was beautiful and appealing, but it didn't have nearly as much to offer as the big city. "What's in Newport that isn't in Portland?" I asked, hoping I didn't sound rude.

"My family's bookstore," he explained politely. "My grandfather recently passed and I inherited it." He leaned down a bit as if he were going to confide in me. "Though, to be honest, I have no idea where to even begin. I was in school to study music."

I smiled slightly. "Can your parents help you?"

He sat up straight. "My parents passed away in a car accident two years ago. I know what my dad would say though: 'Just dive in and do it, Alex. That's the only way you'll learn.'"

Does he have any family at all? I wondered. "I'm sorry to hear about your parents. That's really horrible." I hoped my lack of inflection didn't make me come off as disinterested; I just had no idea what to say, and I still wanted to be alone.

"Thanks. It's been tough, but I've managed. Jack was actually my dad's horse, so I feel like I still have a small piece of him."

"He's beautiful," I said honestly. I began working shampoo through Cash's tail. "Thoroughbred?"

"Appendix," he said, patting the gelding's neck. "Sire was Quarter; dam was Thoroughbred."

I nodded. "Well, have a good ride."

"Will do," he grinned. "See you around, May."

I watched him ride toward the arena, sitting atop his horse as if it were the most natural thing in the world. With a sigh, I returned to the task at hand and rinsed Cash's coat clean to begin braiding.

Nine

AN HOUR LATER, Cash was groomed. I sprayed him down with a coat polisher before walking him over to a patch of grass to graze. Sitting down, I dropped his lead rope and let him wander while I watched Grace and Alex work their horses. I had never seen anyone so comfortable on a horse bareback as the guy I just met. He had a way with it all: subtle cues people couldn't even see; gentleness and grace. It was almost as if he were whispering to his horse in a way that normal human beings couldn't. And he smiled sometimes, though most of the time his eyes were focused and serious.

I wondered why he was so happy after his losses. He wasn't exactly bubbling over with joy, but he had a peace about him that I couldn't place. It had me mesmerized, wanting to have a fraction of it. I wanted even a moment of peace.

I pressed my lips together as tears brimmed in my eyes. Looking down at my lap, the droplets fell onto my jeans and left little dark stains. I felt so lost. Nothing in the entire world made sense. Even my own tears seemed out of place. Shouldn't I have been angry instead? Maybe I was angry. Maybe I was hollow. I felt as though something irreplaceable had been stolen from me, and I didn't even know who to blame.

"No matter what, things are stolen when the owner of them makes the mistake of letting their guard down in one way or another," my mother,

the Criminal Defense Lawyer, once said. *"You leave your door unlocked. You don't install an alarm. You trust people you shouldn't. No matter what, it could have been prevented."*

Was it the same with rape?

I couldn't count the number of times that my mom defended a rapist in court. I was never there to witness it, of course, but she would recount the stories later on. It was never that she was trying to prove them innocent, but she aimed to ensure their sentence was fair. "He's sick, no doubt," she told Dad once. "Clearly dealing with damage caused by childhood abuse. That contributes to his actions."

Were there excuses to be made for such an evil deed?

I picked a dandelion and twirled it between my fingertips. I just needed to move on. Nothing could take back what had happened, and I knew I didn't want to live the rest of my life feeling this way.

Maybe I could convince my parents to transfer me to the public school system, I contemplated. *At least so I wouldn't have to see him again.*

"Is that your little sister out there?"

I looked up to see Alex walking beside his horse across the grass. "Yes. That's Grace."

He smiled. "She was watching you over here. I figured that was the case."

I looked away and dabbed at my cheeks with the back of my wrist. "Probably wondering why I'm not riding."

"Why aren't you?"

"I'm just not feeling it today," I shrugged.

"Mind if I sit with you?"

Yes. "No."

Alex dropped Jack's lead rope and let him graze. He then sank to the grass beside me and took his baseball cap off to wipe the sweat off his forehead before putting it back in place. "How long have you been riding?"

I watched Cash's side twitch when a fly landed on him. "My whole life. You?"

"Two years or so. After my parents died, I took it upon myself to take care of my dad's horse."

He's only had two years to learn to ride like that? I thought. "You're very talented."

"Naw," he grinned, squinting slightly from the sun. "It just makes me happy. Like I said before, it helps me feel close to my dad."

"And your mom?" I asked.

"My mom had this incredible talent for music. I always knew I wanted to study music in college, but after she died, it sorta became my top priority. Sometimes I play some of the songs she wrote."

"Guitar?" I asked.

"Piano," he grinned, turning his face to look at me. "Thankfully, there's an old baby grand in the apartment above the bookstore. That's where I'll be living."

"Sounds like you're set," I mused, plucking a few blades of grass. "Are you going to sell the place?"

He tilted his head for a moment in contemplation. "Not sure yet. I mean, Granddad did alright. He made enough to live on. It'll be a lot of work and I need to decide if that's what I want to devote my life to."

"You could try it for a few years and see?" I suggested.

"Yeah. I think that's the plan. Plus, I'm working on an album. Never know, I might be the next big thing," he winked. I could tell he was being facetious.

I laughed. *Actually laughed.* "Maybe you will."

"May, we're leaving!" Dad called from the parking lot. "Drive safe coming home."

"I will," I called back. I watched them get in the car and leave, and I realized that Alex and I were the only ones left on the property.

"Your family seems nice," Alex said.

I inhaled a deep breath and rubbed my tongue along the split that was still healing on the inside of my lip. I nervously got to my feet. "Well, it was nice to meet you, Alex. See you around?" I offered, retrieving Cash.

Alex stood up. "You too, May." He eyed me for a moment, confused. "See you around."

I didn't look back as I brought my horse into the barn. My hands shook while I took his halter off in his stall. I breathed deeply, trying to calm my crackling nerves. I was being ridiculous, and I knew that. But I couldn't help how acutely aware I was that I was alone with this stranger outside. I jogged to my car, spurs jingling with every step, and left without looking at him.

* * *

WHEN I GOT HOME, Mom's Mercedes was pulling into the garage. I parked behind her and took a steeling breath before stepping out of my Jeep. "Hey, Mom," I said. She draped her stiletto-heeled legs outside of her car to make her ladylike exit. She stood to her full, statuesque height and acknowledged me with a wave because she was on the phone.

"I don't *care* what his lawyer said, John. That woman is clearly lying!" she huffed, taking her briefcase out of the back of her car. She headed inside, still spouting off to her assistant on the other end.

I stood in front of my Jeep and rubbed my arms slowly, flinching when she slammed the door.

"Hey," a familiar voice said behind me.

I turned and met eyes with Danika. Her arms were crossed and she was eyeing me grimly. She tapped her foot. "Since you wouldn't look at me at school, and you wouldn't answer your phone, I thought I'd come talk this out with you in person."

I turned away and started toward the house. "I don't want to talk about it, Danika."

"What is *wrong* with you?" she shouted, catching up to grab my arm. "Why haven't you been at school? And what did I do that was so terrible?"

How could I explain this to her? How could I say I was angry because I was only at that party for her? That I stayed to make sure *she* was safe? That she acted like a child and locked herself away so I *wasn't safe*? And how did I convince myself that none of this was really her fault? "Dani, I'm just . . . I'm not ready to discuss it, alright? I'll see you at school on Monday."

"Is it because the guys like me and not you?"

I whirled around in complete shock. "You think that's why I'm upset? I'm upset because I tried to tell you how beautiful and smart and worth it you are, and you threw it back in my face. I'm upset because while I was being a *real* friend to you, you were off taking me for granted and refusing to leave with me like you promised, so I had no choice but to stay at that God-forsaken party. I'm upset because as smart as you are, you're also the most ignorant and selfish person I know!"

Her eyes watered. "So that's how you really feel?"

"That's how I really feel."

She turned and got into her car without saying another word. I watched her drive away, wondering how she could be so blind. How could she have been just a couple rooms away when Tyler raped me, and witnessed how I acted just seconds after, and still not know? I despised her for her selfishness.

"May? What are you doing?" Dad called from the front porch.

I realized I had been standing there, staring into space. "Coming," I sighed.

Ten

MOM WAS SITTING at the kitchen bar with a glass of wine and a book in front of her. She looked at me over the rim of her glasses when I walked through the front door. "Hello, May," she said, extending an arm to gesture me into one of her stiff hugs.

I complied. She smelled like gardenias. "Hey, Mom."

She returned to her book when we parted. "Did you have a good ride?" she asked. Mom was the type who could read, cook, drive, clean, brush her teeth, make her grocery list, do her makeup and judge you ... all at the same time. I had been quick to learn as a child that I couldn't glaze over the truth when I thought she wasn't listening, because it always came back to bite me. She watched me again, her lips forming a straight line. "What's wrong?"

I told her a little bit of truth and hoped she would think there was nothing more to it. "Danika and I had a huge fight. I'm just feeling kind of down about it."

She assessed me for a moment. "What about?"

Don't mention the party, I told myself. She would only ask more questions about it. "What is it always about? Boys." I tried to laugh but failed. "She's just selfish and manipulative. I wish she would grow up."

"It's a shame, really," she said before taking a sip of her wine. "The girl has so much potential—just as much as you. She just doesn't utilize it."

"Yes!" I said, glad she was taking this direction. I went to the fridge to get a bottle of orange juice. "That's exactly what I was telling her before she blew up at me."

"People like her don't like the truth."

I pretended to look for something else in the fridge. "Yeah."

She didn't say anything. I knew I couldn't stare into the fridge forever, so I closed it and turned around with my orange juice in hand. I brought the juice to my lips in waiting for her to say more, only to hiss when the acidic liquid touched my cut. I almost choked. *Would it ever heal?*

She glanced up at me, one brow arched.

"Wrong pipe," I lied. We stared at each other for a moment before I turned on my heel and walked around the bar. "I'm going to go shower."

"Yes, you do smell like the barn," she said with a note of disgust.

I rolled my eyes as I headed for the stairs.

"And May? I don't want to hear that you went to another party without helping your sister with her homework first. Are we clear?"

Luckily, she wasn't looking at me. If she had been, she would have seen the color drain from my face. "Yes, Mom. I'm sorry."

I climbed the stairs as quickly as I could to avoid further interrogation.

Now

I STARE AT AN EMPTY CANVAS, brush poised in hand, yet I don't know what to paint. I haven't painted in years. Elijah is singing Addison to sleep for her nap in the next room, and I can hear her squealing dramatically now and then. She doesn't want to go to sleep, as usual. She giggles excitedly, but she sounds tired, as if on the verge of giving in.

That sound prompts my brush to pick up a smudge of pink. I begin painting laughing lips; her lips. And around those lips, I paint her perfect, chubby, porcelain face.

I stroke a tiny bit of white over her iris, making it look as if it is reflecting sunlight, just as Elijah's lips graze my neck. "You're painting again," he murmurs happily.

And he brushes my tears away with his fingertips, kissing every inch of my face as he does so.

Then

WHEN MONDAY CAME, I told my parents I had a migraine to get out of going to school. I had been known to have them from time to time, so it wasn't unusual for me. After my dad analyzed my pupils and temperature in order to satisfy himself that it wasn't more serious, I was left with a bottle of water and some Excedrin and instructed to stay in bed.

But I didn't. As soon as they were gone, I tossed my hair into a ponytail and put on the same pair of dirty jeans I had worn to the stable the day before. I pulled on a black hoodie as I left my bedroom, crossing the hall to knock on Grace's door. It was already open and she was making her bed.

"I need a favor," I told her. She looked at me expectantly, so I continued. "I need you to not tell Mom and Dad that I left the house today. I just need to get out."

"I won't tell," she promised, soft-spoken as usual. "Where are you going?"

"Just out." I was going to the barn, but I didn't want to tell her that because I wanted to go alone. "I won't be gone long."

She nodded, confirming she understood.

"You know the drill. Don't answer the door, keep it locked, and—"

"I know, May."

She knew. She had been staying home alone off and on for a year now. "Right. We'll work on your studies when I get home. We can do homework together." I tried to smile and partially succeeded. And when I made my way down the stairs, I realized with a sigh of relief that the soreness in my body was mostly gone.

* * *

CASH WAS PARTICULARLY peppy from not being ridden over the weekend. His ears were pointing forward and his neck was outstretched over the top of his stall door when I approached. I loved that he was always happy to see me, treat or no treat. My lips tilted into a semblance of a smile while I slipped his halter over his face.

A few minutes later, I undid his braids and lugged his saddle out of the tack room to hoist onto his back. The weighty bulk of it settled directly atop the red and white blanket I had placed there first, and I wriggled it into position before reaching under his belly to grab the girth.

I lifted upward each time I laced the leather strap through the loop, securing the girth into place just enough to keep the saddle on his back during our trek to the arena. He blinked lazily while I brought the bit to his lips, and his teeth parted to let it in. When all was set, I led him out of the barn and into the sunshine.

This felt good. All of this. Horses had always calmed my spirit, and it was no different now. Of course there was still a nagging sense of disorientation, since I had yet to learn which way was up and which was down since the night of the party. But for now, I felt safe; free to be open. Cash only judged me on my ability to guide his every step and the way I rewarded him in turn. He didn't know about my inner turmoil, and he didn't need to in order to comfort me.

I patted his neck as his head bobbed contentedly. We went into the arena and I closed the gate behind me before tightening his girth the rest of the way. Grabbing the horn and cantle between my hands, I lifted my foot into the stirrup and climbed on, settling into the saddle before finding the other stirrup with the toe of my boot.

This felt like coming home. Sighing, I ran my fingers through his wavy mane and watched the way it flowed between them like black silk. "Feels better up here, boy," I whispered. "Thank you for that."

I touched him with my calves and he moved forward at an easy walk as I adjusted the reins in my hands. I felt my hips move, swaying ever so gently with each step he took. The movement was therapeutic, as if undoing the days of stiffness that had accumulated there. We went in a circle, using half of the arena before turning the shape into a figure eight.

I squeezed him gently with my legs and he transitioned into a trot. His body curved beautifully with each circle; perfectly tuned movements from years of practice. I could feel myself beginning to forget everything except for how to direct the horse beneath me, our minds unifying until we were engaged in a perfect dance.

Moving my hip forward just enough for him to feel my weight shift, he immediately picked up a three-beat lope that rocked me like a gently swaying boat. As pent up as he was, he was still in tune to my cues, and he listened to them fully. I broadened our circles until we used the entire arena, then shrunk them down again. We repeated this until we crossed directly down the center, and I shifted once more to have him switch leads. His right foot became the leader now as we went clockwise around the rail.

His mane flowed up and down against my hands and I felt his sides gently heave with each breath he took. Moments like this were magical. They weren't ordered by a trainer or expected to be the picture of perfection for a show. We were just a masterpiece all our own to a point where we became a single entity.

Turning abruptly to take flight down the center length of the arena, I urged Cash to let go. And when it was time, I straightened my legs in front of me to give him the signal to put on the brakes. His hind end dropped and we slid to a stop, dirt flying up at our sides. I heard a single round of applause and when I turned my head, I found Alex sitting astride his horse with a beaming grin on his face.

"Can I just say that was one of the coolest things I've ever seen?" he proclaimed, jogging his horse toward me.

I felt my face redden. I only ever rode like that when no one was looking. "He can slide further than that," I explained shyly. "It's been a while since we practiced."

"Well, it looked pretty clean to me, but I'm no expert."

I remembered seeing him ride on Saturday and secretly thought he had to be trying not to come across as cocky. Or perhaps he really didn't know how talented he was. "Well, thank you. No book store today?"

He adjusted his worn-out ball cap with the Portland State Viking symbol across the front and tilted his head. "It's closed until I figure out what to do with it. I'm cleaning it up in my spare time. Granddad wasn't the best with a dust mop."

"I see. How old is the place?"

"It turned fifty-six this year. He opened it when he was my age. Though to be honest, I think he was a lot smarter than me."

Did I just laugh? The sound didn't seem to come from me, but I heard it all the same. "I bet you have his genes. Never know, you could turn that store into something irreplaceable."

He seemed to ponder the idea, blue eyes twinkling thoughtfully. "That's just it though. Book stores are a dime a dozen, and technology is making the demand for real books die away. The store was suffering long before he passed."

I frowned. I felt sorry for him in a way. Though he was smiling, he seemed lost. "Is there no one that can help you?"

"Nah. It's a one man show, I'm afraid."

"That's a lot to try to deal with," I offered, but the words felt recited. Were they the same ones I had been hearing in my own head for several days? "Do you want some help?" *What was I offering, exactly*? I was just trying to be nice, but suddenly I wished I could backtrack.

"I could use a creative eye." His grin was warm and kind. Something about it calmed my nerves.

I took a slow breath and glanced at the surrounding mountains before returning my gaze to his. "I could come tonight after homework," I said softly; meekly. I wondered if he sensed my hesitance.

"In order for it to be a deal, both parties usually offer something," he winked. "How about I supply pizza?"

If he sensed it at all, he wasn't showing it. I still didn't know if I had made the right choice in offering to help him, but nothing about him made me uncomfortable. In fact, though I was confused and hesitant about our plans, I was completely at ease around him. "Deal." I smiled.

"Good. Sure your parents won't mind you helping a twenty-year-old city boy?"

I shrugged. "I'm a senior this year. Besides, it's for a good cause." It felt awkward even discussing the mechanics of a girl my age and a guy his age hanging out, because first of all, this wasn't anything remotely close to a date; I wouldn't be going if it were. Secondly, Alex didn't strike me as the kind of guy who was hiding something.

Then again, neither did Tyler.

My fingers tightened around the reins. What had I promised again? Was this really a good idea? But the look on Alex's face, a look a friend gives when they're looking forward to future plans, made it impossible for me to back out. His eyes were just so *kind*.

Tyler's eyes had never been kind.

And I realized then, as much as I loathed it, that I would likely forever compare every guy I met, platonic or not, to Tyler Jenkins.

"Well, good," he nodded firmly. "I'll be there all night, so stop by whenever you feel like it." He gave me the directions and then rode off to do his own thing, and for the next hour or so, we both shared the arena in comfortable silence.

Eleven

I STOPPED MY CAR by the curb of the old bookstore and looked up at the fading sign that displayed *Adair Books* in white lettering. The place looked quaint and warm from the outside, welcoming me even before I stepped onto the sidewalk. But as I approached the antique wooden door, my heart began to skip erratically. *What am I doing here?* I wondered. I wanted to be locked away in my bedroom, doing my homework without being forced to interact with anybody. But this was normal, right? It was normal to make new friends.

I had expected my parents to be hesitant about me helping Alex, but apparently Dad had already met him at the stable the week prior. Mom was just glad I actually *wanted* to get out of the house. "The medication seems to be working!" She had said this in a way that suggested that now my problems would be solved forever. "Think you'll be up to school next week?" she had added.

Dr. Fletcher had mentioned to her that I wanted to be taken out of school, and while she hadn't addressed it completely, I knew by her commentary that such a thing would never happen. I was the normal daughter: the one with zero concentration issues. I knew she wouldn't be giving up on that belief any time soon.

That's partly what drove me all the way to the door of Alex's inherited bookstore rather than backing out completely. It was time I started pulling myself together or I knew I would be eaten alive by my issues.

As I was reaching for the handle, the lock turned and the door opened. I lowered my hand and locked eyes with Alex, who was grinning at me. His brown hair was short and groomed neatly. He had a smear of sage-colored paint on his cheek and his white t-shirt was tattered and stained by various other paint streaks. Same with his jeans. His black Converse shoes were the only thing left unscathed. I could smell the fumes inside, though the scent wasn't unpleasant; it had always inspired my creativity.

"You came!" He pushed the door open and gestured me inside. "I was just testing some swatches on the back wall. It used to be this awful shade of yellow . . . like baby poop. I don't know what Granddad was thinking."

I followed him, letting my eyes wander around the interior of the store. All of the shelves were old and sturdy, and some of them stretched all the way to the ceiling with rolling ladders attached to a rail. The place felt special; not bland and industrial like most modern bookstores. But it was dim and dusty, and I made a mental note to suggest some decorative lighting.

"Alright, so we have green, lighter green, lighter-ish green, blue, and tan."

I looked at the swatches and felt my lips tug into a smirk. *"Men only see five colors, while women see a thousand,"* Addison once said. *"Kind of like how we see all of our flaws and they only see beauty; the pinnacle of perfection. We'll find men like that one day, but we'll let them just keep seeing those five colors so that we can paint our houses the way we want."*

The thought came from nowhere and I almost forgot to respond. When I did, my own voice felt foreign. I realized at once that I was forcing myself to make conversation. "Well, the green is actually similar to emerald, and I think that's *too* green. The lighter green is closer to sage, and the lighter-ish green is between mint and pistachio. Of those three, I prefer the sage. I think that blue is pretty, but it kind of reminds me of a hospital. And the tan is more terra-cotta, which I think would be good for an accent wall but not for the entire space." I looked at him and found him smirking with his eyes and suddenly I felt embarrassed. I feigned interest in my work boots and tattered jeans. "Sorry, that was probably more than you cared to hear."

"No, actually. I didn't read the labels but I thought the colors were nice. I just don't have the eye for this kind of thing. Sounds like you do."

I chewed on my freshly-mended lip: a habit I had developed ever since the cut closed up.

He was peering intently at the swatches with his head tilted, rubbing his scruffy chin with his fingertips. "So sage all around, and terra-cotta on this wall?" he asked.

"I think that would look really nice. You could even do some texturizing."

"Yeah," he drawled, then laughed. "I have no idea how to do that."

"Me neither," I shrugged. "It can't be that hard though."

Alex was quiet while he continued to examine the wall. I rubbed my arm awkwardly, glancing around the room, though my mind was blank. I felt as if I should fill the silence, but he seemed perfectly comfortable. My feet put distance between us on their own accord.

"Lighter green and tan it is," he winked and passed behind me. I watched him head for the front counter and noticed a pizza box sitting beside the cash register. "I hope you like pepperoni and pineapple!"

I wrinkled my nose and followed him. "Never tried it." When was the last time I had eaten a full meal? The thought of eating was nauseating, but I knew I would have to do it at some point. My clothes were already beginning to hang loosely on me.

"Well, you're in for a life-altering experience." He opened the box and brushed behind me, putting his hand on my upper back in passing. "I'll be right back."

My entire body tightened, all of my muscles binding into knots. *He didn't hurt you and he won't*, I told myself. *Get a grip.*

I breathed out and watched him disappear around the corner. A moment later he returned with a stack of napkins and some paper plates. Setting them next to the pizza box, he glanced at me with a thoughtful tilt of his head. "So, May. Tell me about yourself."

I looked down at my hands and watched the way my fingers tapped lightly on the countertop. I knew me better than anyone, yet I had nothing to say. My mind was blank. Biting the corner of my lip, I recited the same spiel I told anyone else who asked this question: "Well, I'm May . . . May O'Hara." *Obviously.* Blood crept up my neck and into my face, making my skin hot. "I'm a senior this year." Again, obviously. I looked at him and saw his eyes smiling. Did he think I was strange? I couldn't formulate any other words, so I diverted my attention to the pizza and put a slice on my plate.

"I know those things." He laughed lightly and dug in as well. "I know you love horses; that you've ridden your whole life. I know you have a little sister named Grace. And I know you have a knack for choosing paint colors. That's all I know, but surely there's more to May O'Hara."

Why did he want to know about me? Somehow I had thought I would come here, help him, and then leave. But Alex seemed to want to *know* me, and for some reason, that unsettled me.

I lifted my eyes to him and we watched each other for a moment. The sun slanting through the dusty windows made his eyes shine bluer than ever, specks of dust sparkling around him. I had never seen kinder eyes in my life: wide and soft and curious. Who was he? Why did he want to be my friend? "My dad is a neurosurgeon and my mom is a criminal defense attorney. I have hopes of being a cardiologist, or maybe even a cardiothoracic surgeon. I secretly love to sing, but trust me . . . you don't want to hear it."

A slow grin split his face in two as he leaned back against the counter. "I think I do want to hear you sing."

I should have known better than to tell an aspiring musician such a useless detail about myself. I rubbed my lips together and tried to back myself out of this corner. "You don't. I promise."

He laughed. "Well, you sound very intelligent. Your whole family does, really. I have no doubt that you can reach your goals."

"How do you know that?" I asked, even though I knew he was probably just saying what sounded right.

He held up his fingers one by one to count down the reasons. "First of all, your father is a brain surgeon. That's amazing. Secondly, you strike me as an intelligent girl, and if you have him as an influence, and your mom too, then you must have the support you need. Thirdly, I bet you could do all that without their help anyway."

"What do you mean?" I took a bite of pizza just so it wouldn't go to waste, but mostly to keep myself busy. Tyler's face flashed through my mind. *You seem like the type that would take the world by storm and do it mostly on your own,* " he had said.

"You seem strong. And I don't know you all that well, but I could definitely see you in surgical scrubs," he smirked.

I put my plate down because my hands were shaking. Alex watched me and concern furrowed his brow. "Are you alright, May?"

I rubbed my arms as I moved around the counter to stand on the other side, putting distance between us. "I'm fine," I lied, forcing a smile. Something shattered on the other side of the store and I felt my heart slam into my ribs. Alex looked at me, wide-eyed, and tossed his plate onto the counter. He sprinted through the rows of bookshelves toward the noise.

I trembled violently, turning in a circle while I heard my blood whooshing in my ears. *Get out of here*, my instincts screamed. I heard him say my name, but his voice was muffled. He grabbed my shoulders and turned me around, and I buckled at the knees, a strangled scream emerging.

"May, it's alright. A cat knocked a vase onto the floor from the open window." He held me upright at arm's length and watched me, frightened.

If it was just a cat, why was he so afraid? But then I realized I was hyperventilating so hard that the sound was wheezing through my constricted vocal chords. "I have to go," I choked. I backed away so that his hands released my shoulders. Moving past him, I grabbed my purse off the counter and fled for the door.

"May, it's alright. Really, it was nothing."

The way he was looking at me didn't suggest that he thought I was overreacting. He could tell something else was wrong. And I knew it wasn't rational. I knew I had no reason to bolt. But I was compelled to get as far away from him as I could, and that urgency was too strong to fight. "I'm sorry, Alex."

I didn't wait for a response before I pulled the door open, the bell ringing as it swung closed behind me.

Twelve

I WENT TO SCHOOL the next day, functioning only on coffee and anti-depressants. I was still behind on my schoolwork, but I had enough to turn in that I couldn't justify feigning another migraine. Besides, my parents wouldn't have bought it anyway. They had essentially told me that failing school wasn't an option. Their statement had sparked a thought I didn't even know I had, but it scared me to no end because I was approaching the point of not *caring* if I failed. Which meant I would never be accepted into medical school—which also meant that everything I had ever envisioned for my life would be null. It was a slippery slope. And that morning, I was starting to feel an emotion I hadn't yet processed.

I was angry.

I was angry at Tyler for taking my life and shaking it until nothing looked the same anymore. I was angry at *myself* for letting him have that power. So when I saw him in the hall as I approached my locker, I didn't hang my head or let him see how tired I was. All the while I felt his eyes on me, but it didn't make me crumble.

That was the version of me he *saw* anyway. On the inside, I was quivering and weak. Still angry . . . but weak.

"I'm so glad you're here." Addison sidled up to me and opened her locker. She looked at me with sad eyes and stepped closer to whisper. "You know I care, right? I didn't call this past week because

I knew you needed time. I just hope you knew I was there if you needed me, and I still am."

Addison never pried when she knew I wasn't ready to talk. I had never interpreted that as a lack of caring, but the opposite. I knew even when she wasn't calling me that she was thinking of ways to help. "I know, Addi. Thank you."

She looked behind me the same moment I heard Tyler say, "Can I talk to you?"

I turned around and forced my expression to show nothing but disinterest. But the moment our eyes met, I was sure he could see much more. "I don't really have time," I managed. "Class is about to start."

Tyler looked at Addison in a dismissive way. I felt her touch my shoulder before walking toward our first classroom, but she leaned against the wall to keep me in sight rather than going inside. I looked at her for a long moment, feeling like the space between us was insurmountable. She was my lifeline, and death was staring me in the face.

"I wanted to see if you're alright."

The absurdity of Tyler's words caused my gaze to shift to him in shock.

He lowered his voice after inhaling a deep breath. "Look. I know nothing I say can fix what happened. I just wanted to say that that wasn't me. I don't do stuff like that."

If I could have shrunk away into nothing I would have, and it wouldn't have been voluntary. I wanted to stand tall and firm; to show Tyler I was the only one who came out unscathed; that he was the one who should have been wounded. I wondered if he was trying to make me feel sorry for him.

"You haven't been at school. I know that's my fault."

I stared at him, realizing I hadn't said anything. Blinking a few times to clear my head, I made sure I spoke firmly: "Don't think so highly of yourself. I've been sick." My words sounded as bitter and defensive as I felt.

He clamped his jaw shut and his eyes narrowed. "I'm just sorry, alright? I don't know what came over me. And what were you doing in my bedroom anyway?"

My fists clenched. Was he *blaming* me for being readily available? Did he see me as a stone in his path to make him stumble? My eyes watered. My stomach churned. I wanted away from him . . . far, far away. I took a step back and glanced at the clock: two minutes until the bell would ring.

"I don't know how else to ask this." He shifted uncomfortably. "Are you going to report me?"

My eyes snapped back to him in disbelief. "Is that why you're apologizing?"

He looked around at students passing by us. "It's just . . . something like that could ruin my entire future. College, career, everything. Nothing anyone could punish me with would make me feel worse about what I did, May."

What about my future? What about my life? You're not sorry! You just don't want to get caught.

But all I could say was, "I won't." It wasn't to save his future; it was to save mine. I refused to ever be seen as a victim.

Tyler's face washed over with relief.

The shrill echo of the bell had never been more welcome. I grabbed my book and slammed my locker behind me, making eye contact with Addison as I headed with her into English class.

"That's him, isn't it?" she whispered when we approached our desks. "The guy?"

What was she asking? Was she suggesting that Tyler was the one I lost my virginity to, or the one who raped me? Was she asking both? It didn't matter though. A simple nod was all I could offer, yet it was enough for her to sink into her chair as if she were beneath a heavy burden.

"Hey."

I lifted my head and noticed Danika standing in front of my desk. Her appearance almost stunned me. There wasn't a trace of makeup on her face—something I couldn't remember seeing since before we started the 8th grade. Her hair was pulled back in a simple French braid—a far cry from the billowing curls she usually wore. She clung to her books as though they were sacred to her.

"Hey, Dani. You look nice."

She bit her lip. "Can we talk after school? I really miss you."

Had I missed her too? The only person I had really wanted to see was Addison. But seeing Danika now made me miss her in a way I hadn't expected. I missed the way she used to be. I missed being kids, and the way we used to look at life through rose-colored lenses: back when Danika wanted to be pretty *and* smart; back when I thought the best of everyone. I didn't trust anyone anymore. When it came down to it, I didn't even trust Addison enough to tell her the truth: not because I feared her reaction, but because I knew I would have to be open and vulnerable, and even with her, that seemed impossible.

The point was that I missed Danika too. Maybe talking to her would help me grasp at the straws of my old self. "Yeah. Do you want to go somewhere?"

Her eyes lit up. "Maybe the beach? It's supposed to be nice today."

I nodded. "Beach sounds good."

"Seats please," Mr. Cannon commanded of the two remaining students who hadn't settled in for class. Danika grinned and hurried by me.

"Miss O'Hara, last Friday the class took turns sharing the poems I assigned. You're the only one who hasn't shared."

My fingers clenched around my pencil tightly enough to make the wood crunch, but it didn't snap. I felt every eye on me. Mr. Cannon stared at me, one of his bushy eyebrows lifting into an expectant arch. "You did write your poem, didn't you?"

Had I known that our poetry would be flaunted for all within listening range, I would have written something more colorless; more deceptive to how I really felt. I debated lying to him, but I needed the grade. "Mr. Cannon, I didn't realize I would have to read it out loud."

"Precisely." He shrugged his flannel covered shoulders as though I was missing the point. "Had you known, and had the rest of the class known, nobody would have written the truth. So please, do share."

This felt like a cruel trick. I could feel my stomach twisting into knots as I opened my textbook to retrieve the paper I had safely hidden inside. I stood to my feet, clearing my throat as the paper quivered in my hands.

"Through the gauzy glen,
three beats of steel
pummeled the earth
like the cadence of a wounded heart;
like the crack in her fractured worth.

Upward and onward she rode,
spurring the heaving cage
of lungs not meant for this;
of a life bent on rage.

And bones cracked like thunder
when her companion fell,
and nothing could quench,
no, nothing could quell
the longing for the glen…

the place where she could mend."

"Well, that was depressing," someone muttered from the back of the room.

I lifted my eyes to Mr. Cannon and found him watching me intently, his eyes narrowed in thought. Murmurings continued around me but I was trapped under the microscope, wanting to escape whatever it was he was concluding about me. I could almost hear his thoughts churning together like the spokes of a wheel; his ice-blue eyes were dark and focused. What was he thinking about? I slipped into my chair and looked down at the paper in my hands, seeing that I had crumpled the edges in my grasp. When I looked at him again, his shoulders rose and fell with a sigh. "After class, Miss O'Hara. Five minutes of your time."

A couple students snickered. "Enough," Mr. Cannon barked. He began scribbling on the whiteboard with a bright red marker, finishing the title for our next assignment.

I heard none of it until class was over. And when it was, I waited in my seat while everyone else went on their way. Addison whispered that she would meet me by my locker as she passed by me. Mr. Cannon lifted the door jamb with the toe of his loafer and let it swing shut before coming to the front of his desk to lean against it. "I'll be honest with you. Your poem concerns me."

I folded my icy fingers in my lap and looked out the window at a seagull fighting the wind in the distance. "It shouldn't, really," I assured him, doing my best to keep my voice from betraying me. I turned my attention back to him. "It's all metaphorical."

"Well, yes. Of course it is. Most poetry is metaphorical in nature. It was the image it conveyed that concerns me."

I forced a laugh. "I must have gone overboard. I can be a bit dramatic at times."

Not true. But my substitute teacher was temporary, after all. He didn't know me.

"I might have believed you before, but I am under the impression that you are struggling with your health. I don't know your situation, Miss O'Hara, but I feel compelled to encourage you to talk to someone if your circumstance is too much to bear."

I squinted at him. "I'm not going to kill myself if that's what you're worried about."

That same speculative look returned. "We are never immune to pain; try as we might to stifle it. Your poem was brilliant but it was too raw to be dishonest. Please consider talking to one of the school counselors, or someone who might be able to—"

"To what? *Help* me?" I grabbed my book and shoved out of my seat, passing by him on my way to the door. "I guess this means I failed?"

"You passed," he uttered quietly. "You have the makings of a great writer."

I opened the door and looked at him one last time. "Then what's the problem?"

He said nothing, so I left.

Thirteen

I WENT STRAIGHT into the bathroom and locked myself in a stall. I then climbed onto the toilet and sat on the water tank with my feet propped up on the seat so nobody would see them if they came in. Covering my face with my hands, I inhaled a deep breath before the tears began to flow.

What was happening to me? Why couldn't I get over this? I was a statistic . . . just a statistic. This sort of thing happened all the time to women, young and old alike. So why did I feel like I was the only one who had ever been violated?

"I hate him," I whispered into my hands, rocking back and forth. I hated myself for whatever mistake I made that encouraged his violence. I wanted to tell someone, anyone, but I couldn't. I couldn't because nobody would ever look at me the same way. I would forever be the girl who was foolish enough to get into this situation. I still didn't think anyone would believe me anyway. Addison already suspected I was raped; I didn't have to ask her to be sure. I was glad she was patient and hadn't jumped on the question that most would ask out of sheer curiosity.

But part of me *wanted* her to ask, like most people would. Part of me *needed* that open door to step through. Maybe, like with everything else, words weren't needed between us. We always knew what the other was thinking. I knew deep down she was waiting because she knew I wasn't ready.

Would I ever be ready?

The bathroom door creaked open. "May?" Addison softly called.

I didn't answer. The school bell rang, echoing off the walls around me.

I heard her walk across the tile floor. "I know you're in here," she whispered, just before she bent down and peeked under my stall door. We met eyes and she stood back up. "I'm not going to ask you if you're alright, because clearly you're not. But I need to ask you a question."

I inhaled a steadying breath. "Okay."

"Did you tell the police?"

I squeezed my eyes shut. "No."

She leaned against the door, her toes facing toward me. "Did you tell anyone?"

More tears fell as I whimpered a soft, "No."

"Can you come out so I can hug you?"

I hiccupped with quiet sobs while I climbed off the toilet and opened the door. Addison's face was drenched like mine. I crumbled into her arms and we wept together, and I felt as though a part of me, though still broken, was soothed.

Now

I STAND IN THE SHOWER, touching the places on my skin that were once sore from such brutal hands. Sometimes it feels as though the pain has never faded. It had taken a couple weeks, but eventually the bruises disappeared. Even after they faded, I still saw them when I looked in the mirror, and I still do, even to this day. They mock me, reminding me I will always remember what Tyler did. My mom always tells me that I still need time to heal. Elijah always kisses the places that hurt, even though I've never told him where they are.

I step out of the shower and dry off before reaching for my phone. I asked Elijah to take Addison to the beach for a while so I could have a little time to myself. He understood. As I get ready to call him, I notice the voicemail from my friend, Addison. I've never listened to it. She left it after the last time we ever hung out. I can't bring myself to know what she had to say after the fight that ended our friendship. Yet I also can't bring myself to delete it.

Then

THE SUN WAS SETTING on the horizon when I parked my car on the rocky cliff of Agate Beach. Tourists were snapping photos and looking through the telescope at the orange rays and the shimmering water, but my eyes were searching for the person I was meeting. I could barely see her with my palm cupped over my eyes; she sat on a blanket down below, her blonde braid lying over her back. I locked my car and slipped my arms into the sleeves of a jacket as I made my way down the path.

I took my shoes and socks off and walked across the sand. It had been a while since I felt it between my toes. Years, perhaps. The feeling was calming in a way. I still didn't know how this conversation was going to go, and I was nervous.

She didn't see me coming. I sat down beside her and she looked at me in surprise, a smile gracing her lips. "Isn't it beautiful?" she asked, turning her face again to the sunset. The glow made her look angelic.

"It is," I agreed. I put my shoes aside on the corner of the blanket and crossed my legs under me, tucking my skirt between them so it wouldn't blow up in the wind. Danika was quiet in a way I wasn't used to. The tension drifting between us on ocean air was palpable.

She finally looked at me and rubbed her lips together, as if she were trying to contain whatever was on her mind, but she knew she couldn't. "I hate myself, May." Her voice broke when she said my name. "Everything you said to me was true. I *am* selfish and I choose to be ignorant because it gets me attention. God, saying that out loud makes me feel pathetic." She shook her head and sighed. "You *are* a real friend, and I'm not. But I want to be."

Her sincerity was real. But for some reason, I was angry. I ground my teeth together. "I get that, Danika."

Her bottom lip quivered. "You're mad. Why are you mad?"

Because you know something is wrong with me, yet you still choose to talk about yourself, like always. That's what I wanted to say. Instead, I breathed out my anger in one long huff and chose to acknowledge the fact that she was trying to apologize to me. "I'm not mad. I'm just trying to make sense of everything."

She nodded and tucked a loose strand of hair behind her ear. "I've always been jealous of you."

I squinted in confusion. "Why?" *Why would anyone be jealous of me?*

"Because you've always been so strong. You don't conform to stereotypes to make people like you. You're just you."

I almost laughed. "Oh, Dani. You couldn't be more wrong." She looked at me, waiting for an explanation, so I continued: "There are a lot of things about me that are true: I want to be a doctor, and not because my father is one. I study hard and I like to think I'm pretty responsible, but I'm not as strong as you think. I'm not as put together as I make people believe. My parents, and my mom especially, believe I am their carbon copy, but not because I *am*. It's because from the time I was little, I knew I had to measure up. So I do conform . . . just not in the same way as you."

She chewed on her lip in thought, and then nodded. "I see."

I looked at her intently. "The thing is, you don't have to be dumb for people to be attracted to you. You're enough. I've often felt that if I fall apart, I will lose the respect of my friends and family. But you're already a mess," I joked, nudging her with my shoulder. "So stop being one and be yourself."

She laughed. "I'll try. I really will. And I really am sorry about the whole party thing. I was such a bitch."

"You were," I agreed. "But let's forget about that, alright? I don't want to think about it anymore."

She complied with reluctance and changed the subject. "Why haven't you been at school? Have you been sick?"

It wasn't the subject change I had hoped for, but I went along with it. "Yeah. I guess so."

"With what? Are you okay?"

I turned my gaze to the ocean, choosing not to answer her first question. "Getting there. I just hope I can make up my schoolwork."

"Was it mono or something?"

"Yep. Something like that. Don't worry, I'm not contagious."

She exhaled and smiled. "Oh. Good. Well, I'm glad you're starting to feel better."

Danika and I built a bridge that day, though it still needed work to become stable. I didn't know if I could ever really trust her again. At least I knew that if anything good had come from all of this, it was that she was finally beginning to see her worth.

Fourteen

TIME SEEMED TO PARALYZE ME. When I wasn't forcing myself to concentrate during class or spending time with my friends, I was a statue in my bedroom. I tried to fill every waking moment of my day with some sort of distraction, but it only worked for a while before I was frozen by the memories that were still there, waiting to remind me I wasn't getting better. I was only fooling myself.

I didn't know why I couldn't get past it. I was finally getting to the point, after two weeks of nightmares, to acknowledge that what had happened to me hadn't been my fault. Addison had said it a few times: rape was never the woman's fault. Bad things happen to good people. This revelation had helped in ways, because I was able to take most of the blame off of my shoulders. Sometimes I felt almost normal, but it was fleeting. One minute I was fine, and the next it was a struggle to even get out of bed.

"I was raped." I practiced saying those three words in front of the mirror, forcing myself to hear the words, hoping it would somehow help me move on. "I'm still alive. It doesn't change anything. I refuse to let it change me."

But it had already. I'd lost weight and even my tightest jeans were loose on me. I hardly laughed, and even when I did, it was only half sincere. Every single night, I experienced it all over again in a dream, though I wasn't quite asleep. But I was fine. I had to be. I couldn't let Tyler own me.

He hadn't said another word since the day he "apologized" at school. I had no idea if he even looked at me in class because I refused to make eye contact with him. He had moved on to some ditzy sophomore, and she had clearly slept with him on her own accord. They frequently cruised up and down the halls, his arm possessively draped around her. As far as she knew, she had hit the jackpot.

Danika was still heartbroken. Sometimes I wanted to shake her.

I hadn't been to the barn all week. I just didn't feel like riding, but most of all, I didn't want to run into Alex. His last impression of me would likely stick forever. He probably thought I was insane. In fact, he would probably have been right.

The smell of my mom's wine made me feel sick, reminding me of the alcohol on Tyler's breath. Sudden movements from *anyone* startled me. I cried over everything. Danika was beginning to treat me with kid gloves, as if I was an unpredictable child who needed coddling, yet she still didn't want to be the one to do it. I had made up my assignments, but the stress of homework snapped me like a twig if one thing went wrong. Being stumped on a calculus question made me hyperventilate. The medication I was on seemed to do nothing, yet I wondered how crazy I would really be without it. I was spinning out of control, but I was normal on the outside. A little stressed and emotional perhaps, but normal. My parents hadn't even questioned whether or not I needed further treatment, which was probably because I had successfully knocked out two of my college applications without any prompting from them.

In truth, I just wanted to get out of Newport and far, far away from the memories.

It was Friday before I knew it. Two weeks since the party, yet it felt like no time had passed at all. Just like every other day this week, I left school immediately after we were dismissed so I could go home and be by myself. As I pushed through the double doors to step outside, I heard a voice call my name. Looking up, I saw Alex climb the last step. I blinked, confused. "What are you doing here?"

He moved out of the way of the flow of students, then held up a folder. "Delivering some information to the school. Granddad used to offer student discounts and I wanted to do the same thing."

His eyes were always so kind. He wasn't looking at me as if I were crazy at all, but I wondered if he thought it. I wondered why I *cared* what he thought. "That's cool. So you decided to open?"

"I think so." He leaned against the rail and tucked the file under his arm. "Though, to be honest, I was hoping I would run into you again."

I wrapped my fingers around the strap of my book bag and held it closer to my shoulder. I looked at his tattered hoodie and his jeans. His Converse shoes. Anywhere but his face. "Why?"

"Well, something happened on Monday that startled you, and I wanted to make sure you were okay." He didn't say anything until I met his eyes again, at which his brows furrowed. "Was it something I said or did?"

I shook my head, hating the way I felt when I saw the look in his eyes. I felt guilty. He had been so nice to me and I had charged out of his store like a lunatic. "No," I shook my head again, this time more emphatically. "No, it wasn't you. I promise."

He nodded slightly but the crease between his brows remained. "I know you don't know me that well, but I'm a pretty good listener. If you wanted to talk about it, that is."

Why didn't he just assume I had panicked because I thought someone had broken in? Obviously my reaction at his store hadn't suggested something so simple. That would have been too easy. I rocked back on my heels and peered out at the parking lot, watching some students get into their cars while others huddled together in groups to gossip. I knew that one single rumor would be enough to ruin my life. I fidgeted nervously. "I just startle easily, I guess." I looked at him. "Thank you though. You've been really great."

His lips twitched into a smile. "I have? How so?"

My cheeks warmed and I was surprised I even had the ability to blush anymore. I had to admit it was nice to talk to a guy and not be afraid of him or put off simply because he was male, which seemed to be a trend lately. "Just the pizza and stuff. And your offer to listen. I appreciate it."

"Any time. I need friends in this town," he grinned. He leaned away from the rail and tapped my shoulder with the file. "I'm going riding tomorrow if you want to join me."

He always left the ball in my court, it seemed. No pressure. No exchange of phone numbers. Alex was the type of guy, from what little I knew about him then, that I had always felt safe to be myself around. Guys at my school rarely looked above my shoulders when they spoke to me. That's how it felt anyway. So to be spoken to with respect was a welcome relief. To be treated as a friend and not as fresh meat was welcome, too. And that is what caused me to smile genuinely for the first time in two weeks. "Sure. I need to work Cash anyway. I've been neglecting him."

Alex laughed and pursed his lips for a moment, as if he was hoping to tell me something that wouldn't upset me.

"What?" I was still smiling.

"Well, I've taken him out to the arena a couple times this week, just to let him run around while I worked with Jack. I hope that's okay."

I exhaled, relieved. "Are you kidding? That's great. Thank you for that."

"You're welcome." He nodded with a grin and headed for the entrance. "See you there. Ten o'clock?"

"Sounds great. My dad and Grace usually head to the stable around that time. I'll go with them."

After we parted, I went down the stairs and through a group of seniors to make it to my car. After climbing in, I threw my bag onto the passenger's seat and released a breath as I turned the key in the ignition. I was actually excited about something for once: I was excited to know a new person and not fear them.

I was excited to feel something other than sadness.

* * *

I SAT IN THE BACK SEAT of my dad's Lexus with my back propped against the side and my legs stretched out on the black leather. In my lap was my biology homework. "Do you need any help?" Dad asked.

"No. I'm good."

"I'm really proud of you for pushing through your anxiety, May. You've managed to get your grades back in order; I know how much you were struggling."

I kept reading in my textbook while simultaneously listening. "I had no choice," I mumbled. He didn't seem to hear me, continuing his conversation with Grace who was in the front seat. I lost myself in my work throughout the duration of our drive until I felt the familiar crunch of gravel under the car. I closed my book and sat upright, looking out the window at the few cars in the lot. Dad parked next to Alex's Camry and I noticed the Portland State sticker on the back window, peeling around the edges as if it had been there for a couple years. I opened my door and put my legs outside to pull on my boots.

Grace and Dad were already on their way in. I tucked my jeans into my boots and closed the door, waving at Alex when I saw him watching me from the arena. He was lunging Jack in a circle.

"Do you want to ride up the trail?" he called.

"Sure," I answered. "Just give me a minute to tack up."

Ten minutes later, I hauled myself onto my horse's back. I rode out of the barn and jogged Cash up to the arena where Alex was already settling in the saddle on the outside of the gate. He smiled at me and nodded toward the trail. "Ever rode it before?" he asked.

"A couple times. There are a couple steep parts, but nothing too bad."

He smiled and slowed his horse so we were riding side by side. "By the way, I finished the accent wall. The texturizing came out better than I thought."

"Good," I smiled. "The terra-cotta color?"

"Yep. I got a few buckets of the sage color too. Whispering Meadow to be exact."

"Oh, Whispering Meadow," I exaggerated. "How mysterious."

He laughed. "I think you made a good call though."

I bit my lip, weighing an idea in my head that I was a little scared to voice. I decided to anyway. "Well, when you're ready to paint, I'd like to help."

He tilted his head with a happy smirk. "I'd hoped you would say that. I need to get the place up and running so it'll start bringing in money. I mean, I still have enough inheritance from my parents to survive, but I don't want it to run out too quickly."

It was easy to forget that Alex had lost almost his whole family. "You're really brave, you know that?"

He looked at me and lifted an eyebrow. "What makes you think that?"

"Everything," I sighed. "Losing your parents and your grandfather; having to tie up all of the loose ends on your own. It must be daunting and terrifying."

He looked up at the sky. "I won't pretend that isn't true, but I don't get to be terrified, you know? I don't get to drop the ball. This stuff is too important."

"You get to be sad though." I almost cursed myself for saying something so presumptuous, but it was too late to take it back. I watched him for any sign of anger.

"I am sad," he admitted with a sigh. He looked at me with weary eyes, but they only showed his sadness for a brief moment. "I'm just trying to grieve in a productive way."

I admired him and I barely knew him. I wished I had his strength; his fearless resolve. "I know I didn't know them, but I believe your parents would be proud. So would your grandfather."

"Thank you. I hope so." He rested his wrist on the saddle horn and looked at me with a new expression—one that was light and warm. "What do you do for fun?"

What *did* I do for fun? None of my hobbies had ever felt like fun to me. Instead they were a means of expression, and a way to make sense of my thoughts and feelings. "I love to paint," I offered, but skipped the part about losing interest in it.

"An artist!" he beamed. "I knew you had to be. You're a deep thinker."

I almost snorted. "I am?"

"You are."

My cheeks burned. I rubbed my lips together and watched the path ahead. Why did smiling feel so strange? Why did I feel like I was insane for feeling a bit of contentment? Maybe it was because I still felt so broken beneath it all, and that made me feel like a liar. I felt like I was lying no matter what I did.

"There you go again."

I looked at him and found him grinning. I smirked. "I guess I can't help it."

He chuckled, squinting in the sunlight. "So what do you like to paint?"

I shrugged. "Landscapes, mostly. Sometimes people."

"I would love to see your work."

I thought he had to be saying that out of courtesy, but his eyes were completely sincere. I felt nervous for some reason. "Only if you show me your music."

"Done. You just bring your paintings to the shop and I'll play you something. Then we paint the walls."

His suggestion was so hopeful in a friendly way; so unlike the typical manner in which guys had asked me to hang out in the past. I didn't sense that he was looking at this like a date. Had he been, I never would have reciprocated. "Sounds great. When?"

He grinned triumphantly. "Tomorrow morning?"

We rode quietly for a while, though the silence wasn't uncomfortable. I glanced at Alex when I knew he wouldn't notice and watched the way his head tilted back when the sky began to mist. He closed his eyes and exhaled long and deep, a serene look on his face. He really was striking in a gentle and beautiful way. He had a way of calming me as if he were communicating with a scared animal, and he probably had no intention of doing so.

I decided then that I could trust him.

The mist turned into a steady but light downpour. "Should we turn back?" I asked.

He opened his amused eyes and looked at me, water trickling down the bridge of his nose. "Are you afraid of a little water?"

My lips twitched. "Are you?"

His answer was a mischievous grin. He kicked his horse's sides and off they went, tearing down the trail ahead of me. Laughter rolled out of me and disappeared into the rain as Cash and I flew through it after him.

Fifteen

WE STOPPED OUR HORSES along the edge of a pond and laughed at how hopelessly drenched we were. Alex nodded to an enormous evergreen that seemed to have been hollowed underneath its weighty branches. The bows were cut from the trunk, allowing for a space to duck under. Thunder boomed overhead as I slid out of the saddle. We took the reins from our horses' necks and held onto them as we ducked for shelter.

"Isn't hiding under a tree practically tempting fate?" I asked as thunder boomed once more.

Alex laughed and sat on the bed of moss and twigs, resting his back against the tree trunk. "No more than trying to ride back in this. Hey, you're freezing."

I was indeed shivering profusely. Hugging my arms to my body, I tried to get it under control. "Oregon weather," I mused casually. "Sometimes I wish it was a little more predictable."

He held out his hand in a *come here* motion, opening up his side as if to invite me in. When I only looked at him, he tilted his head. "Your lips are blue. You aren't catching pneumonia on my watch."

I felt a small river of water begin to trickle around my knees, serving to remind me there was no escaping the cold. Yet I couldn't bring myself to accept Alex's gesture. "Really, I'm fine." I tried to smile convincingly, but I knew I seemed less fine than stubborn.

When a cold blast of wind swept under the bows, I knew I was going to have to compromise. I crawled forward on my hands and knees and sat down on the damp ground beside him, slowly nestling into his side. His arm closed around me and I felt that he was shivering too. "See? I don't bite." He grinned and rested his head against the tree, his body quivering.

I let my bent legs lean against his and tried to soak up his warmth. "I guess you don't."

"But just for the record, I'm still not afraid of a little water."

I looked up at his smiling face, eyes closed though clearly amused. "Me neither, though my dad is probably freaking out."

Alex hissed through his teeth as if he dreaded that thought. "I'll do my best to explain when we get back. Your dad seems really nice, by the way."

"He is. He could do better in the father department, but he tries. He's just not around much, and when he is, he seems to think I should be just like him."

He opened his eyes and looked at me, serious and thoughtful. "I think everyone thinks that about their parents. My dad was drunk a lot and my mom had a mean temper, but they tried, you know? That's what counts. And when I remember them, I try to remember the good times."

The water in Alex's hair still dripped around his face. His jaw clenched when he shivered. I felt bad that I couldn't offer more warmth. "I think you turned out pretty well."

He smiled. "Dad wanted me to be a contractor like him. I was never interested, but I tried for a while. I wanted him to be proud. After hitting every one of my fingers with a hammer repeatedly, eventually music won. The last thing he said to me was that if I wanted to starve my entire life and perform at rundown bars, he wouldn't stop me. I just wish he would have seen me excel."

He didn't say any of this with sadness in his voice, but it was there in his eyes. "He's proud. You have to believe that."

"I try," he whispered.

I shivered and felt his arm tighten, but I didn't feel confined. I felt safe. "What happened in the accident? I mean . . . if you don't mind me asking."

"I don't mind. They had a fight and Mom stopped the car to get out. She said she wanted to walk home. Dad got into the driver's seat, drunk and stumbling. He picked her up at the next stop sign and floored it through the intersection. They were hit broadside by a two-ton pickup. They died on impact."

I didn't know what to say. The only thing that came to mind seemed inappropriate, but I said it anyway because I had to say *something*. "How do you know all those details?"

He nodded as though he expected the question. "I was in the back seat." He lifted the arm that was around me so I could see his wrist; it was littered with small, white scars. "Shattered radius and ulna. Lots of screws. Punctured lung, fractured neck. Five broken ribs and a crack in my femur."

"Oh my God!"

"It's alright," he assured me. "I was reassembled. This rain makes me ache though."

"But you lost them . . . and you almost lost your life." I shook my head, perplexed at how he could be so strong in the face of all of this. "You couldn't have been completely reassembled."

"I was. Maybe with a few minor flaws, but I can do all the things I did before."

"I don't mean your body." I realized I was fighting tears. How could he not see what I meant? How could he survive such a devastating loss and not be *lost*?

He was quiet for a moment, locked in my tear-filled stare. "I know. You can't imagine how angry I am. He wouldn't let me drive. His selfish choice stole him and my mom from me. I hated him for a long time, May. I hated myself for not finding a way to stop it. But I realized that hating anyone wouldn't undo what had happened. I was consumed by it, poisoned from the inside out. The day Granddad died, I felt that prison open up and release me to live my life. Not by chance, but by choice."

"You chose to live despite your pain."

"Yes."

I envied him. I wanted the resolve he had. My circumstance paled in comparison to his, yet he was so much stronger than me. I hoped that one day I would be able to make that choice and not look back. I looked away so he wouldn't see my tears. "He's proud of you now. He has to be."

"May?" Dad called frantically from somewhere in the distance.

Alex and I looked at each other in surprise. I left his side and crawled out from under the tree. "I'm here!" I called. "I'm alright."

Dad rode through the trees, holding the hood of his bright orange rain slicker tight over his head. "What are you doing out here?" he barked.

He was angry. Alex stood beside me and quickly explained. "I'm very sorry, sir. We went for a trail ride and didn't realize this storm was coming. I thought it would be best to wait for the worst of it to pass before trying to ride back."

He was putting the responsibility on his shoulders. I wanted to intervene, but Dad surprised me by saying, "Thank you. The path is really muddy and slick. I had to ride off the trail. Are you kids alright?"

"We're fine," I promised. "Just a little cold."

Dad nodded. "Let's get back. I don't think it's going to ease up any time soon."

Alex and I mounted our horses. I looked at the path and noticed how the rain had pounded the dirt into rivers of mud. We followed my dad into the trees and jogged the horses all the way back to the stable.

* * *

"YOU'RE PRACTICALLY HYPOTHERMIC, MAY," Dad sighed, rushing my horse to be untacked the moment I slid from his back. I watched him lug my wet, dripping saddle off to the tack room and hugged my body for warmth. "What were you thinking?" he called.

I went to my horse and began wiping the water out of his fur with a curved squeegee. Cash seemed oblivious to the cold, his ears perked and searching for food. Alex tied his horse to the post and brought me a blue hoodie. "Here," he said. "Put this on."

"I can't. It's yours. You're cold too."

"You need it more than me. Now come on."

I did as he instructed and waited as he pulled the hoodie over my head. Then I put my arms through the sleeves and moved my hair out of my face. Alex nodded, satisfied. "Thank you," I said.

"Welcome. Go home and get warm. I'll take care of Cash."

He didn't leave me room to argue before he was jogging off to the same tack room my dad was emerging from. "I'll get her horse, sir. I'm very sorry for all of this."

Dad patted Alex's shoulder in passing. "No worries. Come on, May. Grace is waiting in the car."

I started to take Alex's hoodie off, but he took hold of the hand warmer slit in the front and held it in place. "Wear it home. You can bring it to the shop."

I smiled, though my teeth chattered. "Thank you. See you tomorrow?"

He grinned. "Tomorrow. Nice and dry."

I smirked as I waved goodbye, following on my dad's trail to the car.

* * *

MOM INSISTED I BATHE in her tub; it was enormous and there was a fireplace in the master bathroom. As soon as I was behind the closed door, I stripped out of Alex's sweater and my drenched clothing and turned the knobs for the water to flow. I didn't wait for it to fill before climbing in, gasping from the hot water that burned because my skin was so cold. Soon it began to rise around me and I settled my back against the porcelain, closing my eyes. The fireplace flickered, orange light coming through my eyelids. I was exhausted.

I turned the knobs into the OFF position with my foot when the water was high enough. The shivering had finally stopped, but I ached everywhere.

The door opened and Mom walked in. "I'm going to wash your clothes," she informed me, bending to retrieve them from the tile floor. I knew better than to let them soak the luxurious bath mats she had purchased recently.

"Thanks."

She looked at me and sighed, setting the clothes in a pile so she could sit on the edge of the tub. "You scared me. Your dad called and told me you were missing. What were you thinking?"

"Dad asked the same thing," I sighed. "It was just a lapse in judgment. The sky was clear when we left for the trail." She looked spent, as if she had given all of her energy to worry. It was something I wasn't used to seeing. "We were only gone for an hour, Mom."

"It seemed much longer."

We looked at one another for a moment. I didn't know what to say. "This guy . . . Alex. Do you like him?"

Mom had never discussed boys with me. She looked as awkward as I felt. "He's just a friend. I'm not interested in him."

She lifted one perfectly shaped brow. "You don't have to lie, May."

I hadn't lied, had I? But the way Mom was looking at me as if I were hiding something brought a startling revelation to light: I might have liked Alex. In another time and another place, perhaps.

It was too soon. I knew it would always be too soon. He was amazing. Too amazing.

And all I had to offer was myself: broken, lost, and closed off. Even he couldn't make me vulnerable, even if he did for some reason want more than friendship.

"He's just a friend," I reiterated.

She inhaled a deep breath and resigned with a nod. "I'll wash his sweater too."

I watched her part and wondered if I could even bring myself to go to his shop, as planned, to give it back.

Sixteen

I FELT SICK ON SUNDAY MORNING. I attributed it to the hypothermic exhaustion from the day before. Standing in the shower, my legs were weak and my stomach queasy, and by the time I dragged myself downstairs for breakfast, I was completely drained.

"Morning," I mumbled, passing my mom on my way to the refrigerator.

She marched to her office with a steaming mug of coffee in hand, pausing in the doorway to look at me. "Morning. Did you sleep?"

"I think so." I searched the shelves of the fridge with halfhearted interest before finally settling on a cup of Greek yogurt. I retrieved a spoon and sat at the breakfast bar.

"Don't forget that tomorrow is the twentieth."

I looked at her blankly, confused.

"Dr. Fletcher wanted to discuss your medication after school, remember?" She sighed as though dismayed by my lack of organization. I just couldn't remember such an appointment ever being made. Then again, I was having a hard time focusing lately.

"Oh. Right."

The twentieth: that date sounded important for another reason. Maybe not the twentieth in particular, but a day close to it.

The seventeenth. That was the important day. That was when my period was due.

My mouthful of yogurt sat unmoving on my tongue as my hand paused halfway to the cup. I was late. I had never been late, not even once.

"May?"

My heart hammered like a drum, making my head spin. This was nothing. It had to be nothing! *Maybe it's just because I've been stressed*, I told myself. Stress can cause disruptions in a woman's cycle.

It was then I realized Mom was standing over me, looking at me as though she was examining an alien substance. I remembered to swallow my yogurt and it immediately tried to come back up, but I forced it down. "Sorry, I just remembered an assignment that's due tomorrow."

Bad choice. Since when had I been one to lie to my mother without a missed beat? I was growing reckless. She would see me for the liar I was.

"Oh. Alright," she said, click-clacking her way back into her office.

I put my hand on my forehead and forced myself to breathe. Growing up with a doctor for a father meant medical things were never glazed over. I had talked about my period with my dad more than I ever had with my mom. I knew the facts.

I touched my breasts to see if they hurt. They were sore, but no more than when I had PMS. I realized I had a dull ache in my abdomen like I usually did just before starting my cycle. "I'm just late," I whispered.

Besides, Tyler wore a condom. Pregnancy hadn't even crossed my mind.

"Stupid. You're so stupid, May . . ." I fought the blur of tears. For the first, time I regretted never going to the doctor after it had happened. I could have taken Plan B, and then I wouldn't have been so afraid. But I hadn't; I had buried the facts like they never existed. I had let Tyler off the hook and now I knew I might be paying as a result.

I tossed my yogurt into the trash and felt a sharp cramp twist my insides. Leaning on the counter, I waited for it to pass.

Just as it did, another one hit. I climbed the stairs to my bathroom and pulled my jeans down to check.

The bright red stain was a small victory and a large relief. Exhaling heavily, my shoulders slumped as the tension left my body. "Thank God," I whispered, cleaning up and changing into fresh underwear. I felt even more tired than before, but I figured it was from the brief but intense roller coaster I had just endured. I wanted to go back to bed, but Alex was expecting me. I braided my hair and dabbed on just enough makeup to make me look alive before heading into my closet to dig through my paintings.

I had a promise to keep, and besides, I really wanted to hear him play.

* * *

AN HOUR LATER, I was hauling my canvases to the door of Alex's store, sighing in relief when it opened before I reached it. "Hey," I smiled, sidestepping past him to come inside.

"Here, let me help." He took the largest of them in one hand just before it fell from my grasp.

"Thanks," I answered. I followed him to the counter, where he had already laid the large canvas on its back. He was staring at it quietly.

I leaned the others against the counter and took his sweater off my shoulder, putting it next to the painting. He still hadn't said anything. I looked at him for a moment, and then at the artwork, trying to imagine what he was thinking; trying to see it with fresh eyes. "Do you like it?" I asked shyly, biting my lip.

"Like it? This is incredible!" He looked at me, blue eyes wide and enthralled. "Tell me about it."

His reaction surprised me. I took a deep breath and dove in. "Well, I painted this one this summer. I've always been fascinated with England, ever since my parents took Grace and me there a couple years ago." The painting featured London's skyline. The hues were all bright and smooth with intense brushstrokes that made it look more like a dream than realistic. "It took me a few weeks."

He shook his head, amazed in a way that was still taking me off guard. It was as if he had an original Monet sitting before him. "It's amazing," he said.

"Thank you. Do you want to see the others?"

"Definitely."

I lifted the second of the three and laid it over the first one. The painting showed a girl sitting in the middle of a vast canyon, her face tilted up toward a sky that was pouring rain. You couldn't tell what she really looked like because she was obscured by stormy shadows.

"So full of emotion," he said reverently. "Who is she?"

I shrugged. "I'm not sure. I wish there was some grand story behind it, but there isn't really."

He nodded. "Well, I think everyone feels like this at some point. Secluded, surrounded by a storm. It's very true to life. It's beautiful."

I found it ironic that I had painted something that matched how I would feel months after it was finished. I smirked at Alex. "You know you don't have to lie to make friends."

He looked at me, his eyes serious. "I would never lie to you, May, even if I didn't like them. Brutal honesty is a trait I've always had." He smiled softly. "I'm telling you the truth."

I rubbed my lips together, resisting the urge to look away. Somehow I felt like he was seeing more than my art: he was seeing me, exposed. Brutal honesty. I wondered what he would say he thought about me if I were bold enough to ask, but I wasn't. "Thank you. Okay . . . one more." I picked the last one up and laid it on the stack. "This one was just practice, but I like how it turned out. I wanted to show the blur of a carnival as if it were in motion."

"Well, you definitely succeeded. It reminds me of those time lapse photos photographers take."

I grinned. "Really? That's what I was going for."

"Success." He matched my grin.

Being around Alex was already making me feel better. It was as if he had awoken me from my morning stupor. "It's your turn."

"Ah. Indeed it is." He gestured toward the stairs at the back of the store. "After you."

I led the way up the rickety staircase; it creaked under our weight, but not in a weak way. It was more like the structure was talking to us, revealing its age and memories. I wondered what kind of stories Alex's grandfather could have told about his life here. The top of the stairs opened up into the living area of the apartment, which still had its antique appeal but was newly decorated with things that could only belong to Alex: old records, a couple classical music posters, two acoustic guitars, and various pictures that were pinned to the walls rather than framed. I glanced around quickly, hoping he wouldn't think I was being nosy. My gaze settled on one picture in particular: a little boy with enormous blue eyes and a popsicle-stained grin. The melting treat remained in his grip as he dangled by his feet in the hands of a man that could only be his father. He looked just like him.

And of course, there was the piano. I wondered how this masterpiece had even been hauled to the top floor. Alex went straight to it and sat on the bench, glancing at me over the dark, weathered lid, which was propped up just enough to show the piano's internal parts. I realized I had never really *looked* at a piano before, even having one in my house.

Alex lifted the cover over the keys and it thudded lightly. "I'm working on a song. I haven't named it yet, but I'll show you what I have so far."

"Okay," I smiled excitedly, watching him.

He turned to the keys, his expression shifting. He was thinking. Concentrating. Breathing. It was as though he effortlessly slipped into his true self: the music maker; the person I knew he was even before hearing him play. He stroked one key a few times, a light but haunting intro that built as he began to include more notes. The sound instantly entranced me, making me long for the words that would explain such a deeply emotional sound. And the moment he sang the first words, I felt goose bumps rise on my arms.

His voice was like silk, yet gravelly. Every word was filled with longing:

Stop running, running
Just breathe, breathe, and you'll
Find a way to find your strength
I know I'm meant for more than empty lungs
And an empty heart
So stop running, start breathing
Just start

I closed my eyes when his voice reached a powerfully high octave, a shiver rolling down my spine.

You lost your mind in cityscapes
Forged a path you weren't meant to take
And life turned to death and took you by surprise
But you could stop running

The music faded and I opened my eyes. Alex was watching me. "That's all I have," he said with a slight shrug. He looked back down at the keys, for the first time seeming unable to keep eye contact.

"Cityscapes," I murmured. "That should be the title."

He glanced at me again. "I like that. Come sit down."

I stepped around the piano and sat on the bench beside him, folding my hands in my lap. I kept a little space between us. "Did you write that about your parents and your grandfather?"

He was looking at me now, but I couldn't meet his gaze. I had just peeked into his soul, and for some reason, I felt undeserving of it. "Yeah. I've been working on it for a few months, but I can't seem to finish it. Maybe because I don't feel like I'm running anymore."

I nodded, reaching out to touch the keys so I wouldn't have to look at him. I felt like crying. My heart was throbbing and I didn't know why. "Maybe that could be the transition in the song," I suggested. "Will you play another?"

"Sure." He straightened his torso and rubbed his faded jeans for a moment, thinking. Then he dove into playing as though he didn't even have to find the right keys.

I couldn't stop the words I said,
Couldn't lie to save my life
Here she was inside my head,
The place I've always been alone
She's breathing in, under my skin,
Torn apart, yet held within,
My soul
And I would lie to save my life,
But I don't want to live,
No, I don't want to live alone.

He stopped playing suddenly; the last note was out of place without the next one to follow. Then he turned to me and sighed. "Can I tell you something?"

I braved a look at him. "Sure."

"I wrote this song years ago and it didn't belong to anyone. Kind of like that painting you showed me of the girl in the canyon. I don't even know why I wrote it, but . . ." he trailed off.

I swallowed. "But what?"

He stared into my eyes, his hand slowly lifting to touch my face. His thumb caressed my cheek and sent a current through my body—one that made me freeze, but not in fear. I didn't know what he was doing; didn't know what I should be feeling. But then his face neared mine and my eyes fluttered closed just before our lips touched. It was the briefest kiss, over in a second, but I could still feel it lingering. Opening my eyes, I saw he was still close to me. I was the one to lean in for our lips to meet again.

My head was spinning, bright flashes dancing behind my closed eyelids. I heard him sigh and his other hand cupped my face as he deepened the kiss. I was forgetting. I didn't feel my pain. Just for a moment, I was free. But then I heard Tyler ordering me to stop moving. I broke away, trembling and breathless.

But I was holding it together. I wasn't panicking.

"May . . . " Alex whispered. "Why are you crying?"

I touched my wet cheeks in disbelief, then quickly dried them with my wrist. I couldn't answer except for a simple, "I'm sorry."

He watched me. I could sense he was thinking deeply, trying to put the pieces together. When it seemed like he was going to ask more questions, he exhaled a slow breath. "Don't be sorry. It's okay. Come here." He enveloped me in an embrace that felt safe and protective. "I don't know what you're going through, but I feel that you're hurting. I just want you to know I'm here for you."

That was when my arms went around his waist and clung for dear life, for the first time letting my tears flow without feeling the need to hide them. "And I'm here for you," I answered.

I didn't know what good that promise was. Alex didn't seem to need anyone. But the way he was holding me, though comforting and strong, told me he was thankful for my embrace too.

Seventeen

WE HELD EACH OTHER until both of us were quiet and content. The strangeness of this new embrace had been replaced with something that felt like coming home. We pulled apart slowly, and my heart was calm. I was calm. I looked into Alex's eyes and smiled, but he still seemed concerned. He moved my hair away from my forehead with his fingers. "I know you're dealing with something. You can always talk to me."

It was as though we had crossed the bridge from acquaintances to something much deeper, but to my surprise, that didn't unnerve me. His statement worried me though. What would he think if he knew the truth? I didn't think I could handle putting my trust in someone only to be discarded like a bag of trash. "I know," I said softly.

He tilted his head, his eyes soft and gentle. "What are you thinking about?"

I was wishing I could be overflowing with butterflies. I wished that Alex's touch made me giddy, like it would have under any other circumstances. I wished he had been my first kiss instead of Tyler. I wished I knew what this meant for us.

I wished I knew if I was falling for him, or if I was just mistaken because I had nothing to compare him to except someone who only wanted to use me. Was I just hungry for true, honest affection? Was I just enthralled with Alex because he made me feel safe?

I considered telling him to never kiss me again, but then I realized I would miss it. I would miss him.

"I'm thinking I want to know you even more than I do now. I, um . . ." How did I say it? What were the right words? "I really liked that, but . . ."

He contemplated my words with a thoughtful nod and I knew I didn't have to say more. "You want to slow down."

I chewed on the inside of my cheek. "Yeah."

"Was it too soon?"

I shook my head. It wasn't too soon. It wasn't too much. "I just don't know what to feel about things lately," I said honestly. "I've had a lot going on . . . and . . ." Why were words so difficult? I felt like I had to tiptoe around the truth, yet he wasn't even asking for it. He hadn't asked once.

But he had told me his truth: about the wreck, and through his songs. He had told me the truth from our very first conversation. Suddenly I felt as though the words were there, choking me in their efforts to reach my tongue. Tears pricked my eyes when I felt him lay his hand on my back. "I went to a party a couple weeks ago, and a guy there . . ." I felt like I was going to throw up. I gulped for air, soothing the feeling. *Just say it, May. Say it before you're in too deep, so you can weed him out of your life if he is going to run.*

His hand fell away. "Are you dating someone?"

The words caused me to inhale sharply, my gaze leaving his. I laughed nervously and glided my fingertips across the ivory keys. "No. I'm not dating anyone."

He shifted to face me even more, running his hand through his hair as he cocked his head in confusion. "Did something happen? Something bad?"

The question had been so gentle and safe, stated in a way that begged an honest answer without demanding it. How was it possible that I wanted to run to him and away from him at the same time? "I was just in the wrong place at the wrong time," I explained as casually as I could. I didn't want him to take it too seriously; I just wanted him to have a basic understanding of where I stood.

He took my hand. "May, look at me."

I did, reluctantly. His jaw flexed. I wondered if he was angry.

He seemed to struggle with what he wanted to say, but eventually the words came. "Do you want to talk about what happened?"

"I mean, what is there to say?" I answered, shrugging it off as though he should too. His face didn't suggest he would let it go so easily. I decided that too much had already been said to leave him hanging. He cared, perhaps too much. With a sigh, I continued: "A guy took advantage of me at the party. It's not that big of a deal though, Alex," I promised him when I saw his jaw muscles twitching angrily. I knew he wasn't angry with *me* though. "I'm fine. Look at me. I'm *fine*. He was just high, and like I said, I was in his way."

"May . . ." His voice shook like a spinning top on the verge of falling over. "Did you tell anyone? The police? Your family?"

I shook my head. "I didn't think anyone would believe me. By the time I realized I needed to, it was already too late for them to . . . you know . . . collect the evidence . . ."

I hated that my admission had caused him to be sad. All this time he had been so happy, even though his own life was a stormy sea. I squeezed his hand, wanting him to know I was alright, even if it wasn't entirely true. He was trembling. "It's okay, Alex. Really. I'm okay."

He didn't believe me. I could see it in his eyes. He displayed on his face the very things I truly felt: sadness, confusion, and loss. It was like he was feeling *everything* I was. How was that possible? How could this man possibly be so understanding without having walked in my shoes? He looked like he wanted to cry, but he didn't. Instead he put his arm around me and pulled me into his side. He held me like he was protecting me from the world, and it was in that embrace that I truly felt safe to *feel*.

"You're right. I'm not okay," I whispered. I wrapped my arm around his back and held onto his t-shirt in my clenched fist. "Sometimes I think I am; other times it feels so fresh."

"It *is* fresh," he told me, his cheek resting on top of my head. "I'm so sorry."

Tears escaped and stained his shirt as we clung to each other all over again. "Can I ask you something?" I eventually inquired, lifting my head to look at him. His blue eyes were stormy and devoted. I almost couldn't choke out the words. "Why do you care so much?"

He smiled sadly and sighed. "Why don't people care more? Sometimes I think I feel things too deeply, but I can't help it. And you're someone who's quickly become important to me. I want to be there in whatever way I can."

"Who was there for you?" I asked tearfully.

His eyes flooded. It took him a moment to blink the water away. "No one."

I placed my hand on his cheek and our gazes locked. "Well, I'm here." His eyes softened when his tears broke loose. "I'm here," I said again.

I kissed him then. I tasted the salt of his pain on his lips. He was motionless at first, seemingly hesitant to comply, though he soon exhaled and brushed his hand into my hair. I heard him whisper my name; felt him kiss me in a way that was soothing and safe, unassuming and gentle. Because of this, *I* was the one to fall into him, wanting to be deeper in the safe haven he was offering.

He met my every movement, but he never took it a step further. He was the one who eventually took my face in his hands and gently broke the contact of our lips. He seemed pained to do so. "It's fresh, May. We have time."

I knew he was trying to spare me from regret, or that he was hesitant to bring back painful memories. I wanted to refuse this noble deed. I wanted this feeling to never end, because for the first time, I didn't feel *him* all over me. I only felt Alex, and the difference was that I felt him to the very core of my being where the pain had been residing for two weeks. Now, I felt nothing but relief.

But I trusted him. I trusted I could still return to this place of peace any time I wanted. I trusted he wasn't rejecting me. I don't know how, but I *trusted*.

"Okay," I finally said. "Will you play another song?"

He straightened toward the piano and brought his hands to the keys, instantly playing with such fluidity that no one would ever know he still had tears in his eyes. "Another song for another painting?" He still managed to grin at me through his sadness.

My heart ached in a way that told me that regardless of *why* I was falling for him, I simply was.

Eighteen

Now

I WASN'T RAISED in a religious family. So, my decision to wait for marriage before having sex wasn't because of some purity spiel given by a church. I wanted it because I didn't believe that sex could ever be casual. I knew in the core of my being that the man I would marry would be the only one who could have that piece of me. So when it was stolen, I felt like all of my efforts were null.

I wondered after Tyler raped me what good it was to even try anymore. But the thing was . . . Elijah never saw me as tainted. He never thought even once that some other guy had that piece of me. And he knew how important that hidden desire of mine had been after I revealed it to him on one of our first dates.

And he waited for me. He waited until we entered the room of our honeymoon suite, where he gently, compassionately, and lovingly peeled away the layers of my clothing and my fear. He whispered over and over how beautiful I was, and how much he loved me. He showed me for the first time what intimacy should feel like. I trusted him fully, even before that night.

Because he waited for me, even when I didn't want him to, I knew I was valued. I was worthy. And now, nothing can ever take that away from me.

Then

I PUSHED THE ROLLER up and down the wall, watching the color of Whispering Meadow coat the porous surface. Alex had told me I didn't have to paint; that if I wanted to talk instead, he was willing. But I didn't want to talk, at least not about the same thing. Enough had been said.

"What's the craziest thing you've ever done?" I asked, standing on my toes to make the roller reach higher.

Alex rummaged around with supplies behind me before answering. "Crazy dangerous or crazy *crazy*?"

I laughed. "Crazy dangerous, or daring. I can't picture you *being* crazy."

"Good." He laughed too. "Well, I have gone skydiving and bungee jumping a few times. Does that count?"

I turned around, my jaw agape. "Does it *count*? I'd say that's pretty daring. You couldn't get me to jump off of . . . or out of anything."

He bit his lip, grinning. "I couldn't?"

I shook my head. "You'd have to throw me." I imagined standing on a tall bridge, trying to convince myself to leap off. Even just imagining it made me feel unsteady on my feet. "What does it feel like?"

"Well," he began, dunking his roller in the paint. "Bungee jumping is an enormous rush. There's nothing like it."

"I never took you for the adrenaline seeking type."

He pushed his roller over the wall. "I wouldn't say I seek it. Dad took me to do both when I was a kid, and I guess you could say I was hooked. I haven't done either since he died though."

I watched him for a moment. He was lean and muscular; not a bodybuilder, but still built. He really was beautiful, and not just in the physical sense. "What is skydiving like?"

He paused, a smile gracing his lips. "The initial feeling after jumping is really intense, but then you feel like you're flying. You see everything for miles and miles, and for a few minutes, you feel like you could go anywhere." He looked at me, eyes twinkling.

"That's beautiful," I murmured. I bit my lip, glancing at him. "Alex . . . have you ever heard the 'bird or fish' metaphor?" I instantly froze up. Why had I asked that? Why in a million years would I ever want to even think about that question again? Maybe it was because I wanted to hear him say it: I wanted him to say what I already knew he was. I wanted to feel like it was possible to feel free again.

"I have," he nodded. "My psychology professor brought it up once. Birds are independent, strong thinkers who don't let life, or the storms *in* life, hold them back. They are free spirits. Fish stay—"

"On the ocean floor. They're afraid to be off on their own. They go with others like them."

"Right. Each have their own thing to contribute to the world. Why do you ask?"

I chewed on the inside of my cheek and avoided looking at him. I wished I had never brought it up. "I was just wondering what you think you are."

He contemplated my statement, tilting his head. "I would say I've been a bit of both at times, but lately I feel more like a bird."

I didn't say anything. I could feel him looking at me as I used a small brush to edge along the trim of a window. I knew he was waiting for my side of this equation, so eventually I spoke up when he didn't stop watching me. "I used to think I was a bird."

Could a bird and a fish really see each other eye-to-eye? Was I only fooling myself? Was *he* fooling *himself*? Alex took my arm and gently turned me around. "You still are. Don't let anything change that."

"I just . . ." I sighed, overwhelmed. "I don't want to let it change me, but I've been so lost. And I feel foolish for letting one thing like this disrupt my life. I have so many things I want to do; so much I want to accomplish."

"I know. And you ultimately have a choice about whether or not you'll remain tied to this memory. But May . . . it's been two weeks. You get to feel whatever you need to feel to find your way again."

How did he always know what to say to put things into perspective? I sighed, smiling softly. "You're really perfect, you know that? I mean, what kind of guy would say these things? Would make me feel alright like this?"

"I'm not perfect." He shook his head. "I care. I think we met each other at just the right time."

I couldn't speak for him, but I knew it was true. I had needed to know I could trust someone outside of my small circle of friends. I needed to know that a guy could treat me with respect. I was just afraid of being so broken that I would be the one to hurt *him*.

"Can you show me how you do the trim so perfectly? I think my hands are too shaky," he smirked, looking down at the brush I was still holding.

"Don't you need steady hands to play music?" I teased.

"They're only shaky around you."

I rubbed my lips together and fought a smile, turning away before my face turned too red. Our circumstance wasn't normal. Part of me felt like there had to be something wrong with me that I would enjoy Alex's company after what had happened only two weeks before. Shouldn't I have been cowering in a corner somewhere? Shouldn't I have been afraid of him? I just wasn't. I didn't know why, but I felt better with him than alone.

The rest of the morning was perfect. I showed him how to paint around the trim. We laughed a lot. We exchanged phone numbers. For a while, it was almost like neither of us was wounded. Until the end, at least, when he looked at me as I was getting ready to head back to my car. It was like he didn't know whether or not to kiss me, so I stood on my toes and showed him he could.

* * *

ADDISON WAS THE FIRST person I told. She was also the first person to voice her concerns. "Isn't it too soon, May?" she asked over the phone. "I really think you should talk to someone—maybe a professional—before you think about dating anyone."

I was glad she couldn't see the look on my face: one that would have shown how appalled I was that she would suggest I needed professional help. I rested my hand on my cramping abdomen, reminded that my period would be hitting full-force soon. "Only I can decide what is too fast for me. It's not like he's my boyfriend or anything . . . there's just something there. He makes me feel better."

"And that's exactly how I know this is too soon! I'm no psychologist, but I know how lost you've been up until this conversation. He's not a remedy; you know that, right? I'm just afraid of how this might turn out if you are lying to yourself."

"I'm not lying to myself!" I snapped. "I thought you'd be happy for me."

She sighed. I knew she was trying to arrange her words before saying them, so I let her. "I am happy that you're happy," she finally breathed. "You have no idea how good it feels to hear this joy in your voice."

"But you think it's not real joy." My words were strangled with tears. I sat up on my bed and they fell. "It's not like I'm back to my old self, Addi. I know he's not the solution. I don't even know what he is. I've just never felt this way and . . ." I shook my head, confused. Was she right? Were my feelings merely a way of ignoring my pain? I just didn't believe that was true. "We just have a connection. We understand each other."

"And that's great," she agreed. "Just be careful. And I know you don't think you need to talk to anyone, but it really might help."

"Any therapist would have to report what I tell them since I'm a minor. No thanks. There are plenty of self-help blogs these days."

I couldn't see her face, but I knew she was frustrated. She sighed again. "Enough of this. Do you want to go get some fro-yo? I miss you."

I looked at the clock; it was two: the perfect time because it wouldn't be too busy. I was craving something sweet. "Yeah, that sounds good. I miss you too."

* * *

I WALKED INTO the frozen yogurt shop in a haze. A wave of fatigue had hit almost instantly after getting off the phone. Addison was waiting for me and we smiled at each other as I approached.

"Hey," she said, hugging me. She was dressed in yoga pants and a baggy t-shirt, her hair tossed into a messy but perfect bun. Even without makeup, she looked so pretty. It was effortless for Addison. Sometimes I wondered if she thought the same thing about me. I never felt pretty. I felt especially ugly as we waited in line for our yogurt, with my stomach painfully bloated and my clothes hugging me a little too tightly. I had always had terrible periods. This one was taking the cake already.

"Your boobs are huge," she whispered. "Are you wearing a different bra?"

"No." I shook my head, adjusting the top of my tank to cover them a little better. "I started this morning."

She nodded casually. "I mean, it's not a *bad* thing," she smirked. "What do you want? It's on me."

"You don't have to do that," I insisted, reaching into my purse for my wallet.

"Shut up. You're clearly PMSing and I feel bad for being insensitive."

We looked at each other and started laughing. "Okay, fine. But I'll get it next time."

"Deal. So, you and Danika seem to be doing better. Did you guys work it out?"

"I think so. I mean, we haven't been quite the same since the party . . . but that's probably my fault. Even though she's working on herself, I still can't forget she . . ." I sighed. I didn't want to say it.

"She was the whole reason you were there," she said, looking up at me. "I get that. I do."

I nodded. It was our turn next. "Sooo," she mumbled, smirking at me. "Tell me more about Alex."

I chewed on my lip. "I met him at the barn the weekend of the party. He was so nice and respectful. He's a musician. He played for me this morning . . ."

I realized I had trailed off when the brunette in a white paper hat tapped her pink, chipped nails on the counter. Addison jumped in and ordered hers: plain with fruit and nuts. I asked for plain too, but with roasted coconut and chocolate.

"You hate coconut," Addison reminded me as we stepped to the side to wait for our order.

I shrugged. "It just sounds good. Anyway, he played for me this morning and it was just . . ." I didn't even have the right word for it. "You know that feeling you get when you are lost in your dance routine? I've never felt that before, but I think this must have been close. He played piano and sang his own songs. I've never heard a voice so beautiful."

She nudged me with her elbow playfully. "I think you might just be biased."

"I'm not!" I insisted. "You should have heard him. It was incredible."

"I'll bet. What else?"

We took our yogurts when they were ready and headed for the only available table. The chair wobbled when I sat down and I slowly made it rock back and forth while I thought of what to say. I knew enough about Alex already to tell Addison plenty of things, but somehow I didn't feel like it was my place to tell her about his parents. I scooped the tip of my spoon into the frozen cream and sighed. "His grandfather used to own a little store called Adair Books. He passed away recently and Alex inherited it. So he's taking over until he can figure out what his plan is."

Addison's eyes widened. "How old is this guy? That's a huge responsibility . . ."

"Twenty," I mumbled, shoving my spoon into my mouth. My friend tilted her head as if to ponder the age gap. "It's only three years," I reminded her. "And it is a huge responsibility. He had to leave college early and he has no one to help him figure this out."

"Not even his parents?"

I rubbed my lips together, wishing I could change the subject. But by now I knew Addison already suspected there was more to the story. "Don't tell anyone, alright? I don't even feel like it's my place to say anything." I looked at her and felt an ache in my chest before I even spoke the words. "His parents died a couple years ago in a car accident. He doesn't have anyone. No siblings, no close family. But he's so strong, Addi. I wish I was as strong as him."

She frowned sadly. "I think that's maybe part of why you're drawn to him. He's strong. He sounds like a great guy."

She seemed to really mean it. I smiled and took another bite. "Anyway," I continued after I swallowed, "I don't know what's going to happen. Logically, I know this might be crazy. I mean, why am I letting a guy in right now? Everything in me wants to avoid any and all men. I don't trust any of them; even the ones I know wouldn't hurt me. They all remind me of Tyler. But not Alex. I don't want to label whatever it is we have. I just . . ."

"You feel safe." She smiled softly and reached across the table to squeeze my hand. "And that's great. It really is, May. Maybe he will help you move on. But remember he can't heal you, and the moment you try to let him, you will only fall apart more."

"What do you mean?" I shook my head. "I don't see how that's possible."

"No one can do this for you. You can only heal from the inside out."

"I'm trying, Addison," I swore. "But why can't Alex be there all along?"

What was I saying? What if he didn't *want* to be there long term? What if I really was lying to myself?

She let go of my hand and rested her head on her balled fist, her gaze honest and loving. "He can. But I'm trying to remind you that even if he isn't, you need to be at a place where that's okay; a place where your identity isn't resting in his hands."

The words "you need" made me feel defensive. How did anyone know what I needed; even Addison? But then I reminded myself *this was Addison*. "I'll make sure of that," I promised. Inhaling a cleansing breath, I nodded my thanks.

Nineteen

A LOUD DING THRUSTED me awake. I blinked a few times at my alarm clock, seeing 6:44 in blaring red numbers. It would go off at 6:45, so I reached for it quickly to prevent the obnoxious buzzing. It took me a moment to figure out what had made the noise, but then my phone lit up with a reminder that I had a text message. Alex. I bit my lip and swiped my finger across the screen.

> *Alex: Good morning. Just wanted to tell you to have a good day at school.*

I smiled and settled back onto my pillows, holding my phone above me to reply.

> *Me: Thank you. What are you up to today?*

He called me a second later. I grinned and brought the phone to my ear.

"More painting," he said. "I have to meet with a financial advisor later to try and figure all of this out."

"Sounds stressful," I frowned.

"Nah. Could be a lot worse. I hope I didn't wake you."

"You did, a whole minute early. But it's okay," I smirked.

He laughed. "Hey, do you want to do something tonight? Nothing too late, of course. I know you have school tomorrow."

My stomach fluttered. *"I'm having a party tonight. Nothing huge. Just thought it would be cool to eat lots of junk food and play dumb games like Apples to Apples and Pictionary,"* Tyler's voice echoed in my mind. I forced it away, but the sick feeling that came with it was still there. "I don't think my parents will let me," I explained regrettably. I wasn't lying: school nights were usually off limits. But I wasn't prepared for the regret I felt in telling him no. I reminded myself how much I really trusted him. Running a shaky hand through my bedhead tangles, I released a slow breath. "But it sounds fun. I'll ask."

He didn't respond for a moment. When he did, he was careful with his words. "If you'd rather not, I'll understand. I don't want to rush you into anything."

"I know," I assured him. "And that's why it's not too soon."

"I'm glad you feel comfortable with me. And you really won't be out late. I just want to show you something; a hobby I forgot to tell you about."

"Is that so? Just how many facets do you have, Mr. Adair?" I inquired, smiling. Inwardly, I wondered why I felt like crying.

"Jack of all trades; master of none," he answered with a chuckle. "Ask your parents first. I don't want to get you into trouble."

"I will. Talk to you later?"

"Sure. Text me any time."

"Okay." I hung up and laid the phone on my chest, feeling my pulse roar. It wasn't that I was flustered. It wasn't even that I was excited to hear from him. It was because I felt waves crashing in my stomach, unlike the butterflies I should have been feeling. It wasn't until I was throwing the blankets off of me that I realized I was going to throw up.

"Easy, kid," Dad told me a minute later after I flushed the toilet. I was crying but I didn't notice it until I noticed his presence. I laid my cheek on my arm and felt Dad touch my back. "You alright?"

"Yeah," I mumbled. "I'm feeling better now, I think."

He gently massaged my shoulder. "Are you stressed about something? The medication seemed to be helping you . . ."

I hated to think I was relapsing back into the state I was in the preceding days after Tyler's attack. I tried to convince myself it wasn't Alex. If anything, he made me feel better. Then again, I was so confused by everything that I was finding my emotions betraying me. "Just cramps," I assured Dad. It wasn't, but I knew it would give him an answer.

"Alright. I'll get you a glass of water."

When he left, I locked the door and pulled a tampon out of the cupboard. But when I pulled my pants down to find my overnight pad clean, I felt everything in my chest cease function. Usually by day two, I could barely keep up with it. But there was just . . . nothing.

I frowned deeply, bewildered. I felt weird. There were no cramps; just a deep, full sensation. I touched my abdomen and tried to solve what was happening. Was stress disrupting my cycle? I closed my eyes and tried to feel everything going on in my body. My chest was sore; I touched my breasts and found them tender.

The hope I had found the day before upon the beginning of my cycle was slowly beginning to fracture like fragile glass. I didn't want to consider the alternative.

"May? I'm putting the water on your dresser. Make sure you drink it."

"Thanks," I choked.

I needed to talk to Addison.

* * *

MY LEGS WERE ALMOST useless when I stepped out of my Jeep in the school parking lot. I couldn't even remember the drive there. Addison was walking up the stairs to the entrance and my voice rang out before I even knew I was about to speak. "Addison!" I called. She turned and saw me, a frown clearly visible on her face even from a distance. When she approached, I moved my concrete legs to try and meet her halfway. "I need to talk to you."

"What is it?" she asked, worried. "Are you alright?"

I looked at her in a daze, and then down at my watch. We had ten minutes before our first class. I nodded to the side of the parking lot where nobody would hear us talking. She followed me, and I slowly turned around. "I . . ." I was losing my nerve, so I tried to spit it out. "I think I might be—"

"Hey! What are you guys doing?" Danika called, heading toward us.

I exhaled, frustrated. Danika didn't know about any of this, and I wanted to keep it that way. Addison looked at me, questioning me with her wide, brown eyes. "Do you want to talk later?" she whispered.

Tears tumbled down my cheeks. Whether I liked it or not, Danika was about to know my secret too. "No, I need to talk to you now."

"May, what's wrong?" Danika asked.

I shrugged my shoulders in surrender. I just didn't care anymore. "I was raped at that party, Dani." I ignored the look of horror on her face and diverted my attention to Addison. Focusing on her, I drew the strength to continue. "And I think I might be pregnant."

Addison's face paled. She grabbed my hand. "It's going to be okay," she promised. She looked strong enough for the both of us.

"Oh my God . . ." Danika whispered. "Oh my God!" I looked at her again. Her eyes held enormous, unshed tears. "This is all my fault," she breathed, covering her mouth.

I didn't know how to react. I didn't know what to say. So I stepped forward and hugged her, my fingers still laced with Addison's.

"It's no wonder you hate me," Danika sobbed. "I'm so sorry."

"It's not your fault," I whispered. It would have been easy to continue blaming her for dragging me to that party. In all honesty, I doubted Tyler would have attacked me anywhere else. It was a fluke; something nobody could have predicted. I couldn't put that on her.

Addison joined the embrace. And even though we were all reduced to tears; even though I wished that neither of them had to know any of this, I was still grateful I had them to lean on.

After a while, we all pulled apart. "We'll get you a test after school," Addison said. "And if you want us there, we'll all find out together."

I glanced at Danika, seeing her nod in confirmation. "Okay," I whispered, taking a deep breath. I just needed to find a way to make it through school.

* * *

I PULLED UP MY PANTS and laid the stick on the counter, watching the test strip become saturated. One line darkened in the control window, as well as a negative sign in the test window. My hands shook as I checked the instruction sheet from the box again. "Guys!" I said, opening the door. "Only one line."

I held the sheet out to Addison so she could look at the diagram. Danika stood quietly behind her. She hadn't said a word all day.

Addison smiled, but that smile soon faded. "Wait, it says to wait two minutes before you read it."

My relief dissipated as I stood there for a moment, my back to the test. "Can you watch it? I can't do it."

She nodded, squeezing my wrist as she passed by me. There was nothing but silence for a while. I heard my own heartbeat in my ears. Danika and I were watching each other as if we were both waiting for a bomb to stop ticking. "Any change?" my voice quivered over my shoulder.

Silence.

"Addison?" I asked, turning around. I saw her reflection in the mirror, and it told me all I needed to know. My hand went to my mouth as she faced me, the stick in her hands.

"There's a plus sign."

"Tell me you're kidding."

She shook her head. "I wish I was."

I snatched the test out of her hand, staring down at it as I tried to make sense of the two blue lines that intersected in the middle. They stared me in the face, mocking me. I shook it a few times, blinking back tears. "No, no . . ."

"You can't change the result, May. You're pregnant," Addison stated, taking hold of my arms. "Look at me. It's going to be okay."

"It's not!" I sobbed hysterically. "What did I do to deserve this?"

"Look at me," she demanded again, lowering her head until I lifted my eyes to hers. "You didn't do anything wrong. None of this is your fault. Take a deep breath, okay? Come on, let's go sit down."

I numbly followed her to her bedroom where the three of us sat on the edge of her mattress. She took the test out of my hand and tossed it in the wastebasket by her nightstand. "What am I going to do?" I whispered.

She took my hand. "You have time to figure it out. Nothing has to be decided today. I think you should just go home and process this for a few days."

"No," I shook my head. "No, I have to get it out of me. I want it out." The edge to my tone surprised even me, but I couldn't escape my desperation to make this whole situation disappear. I couldn't believe this was happening to me. It felt like a cruel trick.

"May, don't do anything rash. You're distraught right now. You need to think this through . . ." she begged. "You don't want to do anything you'll regret later."

"I regret getting raped!" I shouted, standing up. Danika gasped sharply. Why was she crying? I stared at her for a moment, questioning that very thing. Challenging her. *How dare she?*

Addison stared at me with her mouth open, but no words were coming out. I decided to spare her the obligation of speaking because talking about it was only making me feel worse. "I have to go. Alex is waiting for me." I opened the door and the sounds of her family conversing filled the room. I grabbed my coat off of her dresser, shrugging into it. With a deep breath, I calmed my tone. "I'll call you guys later, okay? Thank you for being here for me."

Addison came forward and carefully brought me into a tight embrace. "It'll be alright. I promise."

The thing was, no matter how many times she said that, I had an impossible time believing it.

Twenty

ALEX HAD INSTRUCTED me to meet him in the parking lot at Agate Beach. My stomach was in knots the entire drive there and my knuckles ached from strangling the steering wheel. All the while I had fantasized about scenarios that entailed a sudden miscarriage or a falsely positive test. I almost started to believe that something could be the case until I parked my car and saw Alex grinning at me with a large backpack over his shoulder. He brought me back to reality.

I was pregnant. And it only served to remind me that Alex couldn't fix me. He couldn't make this disappear. It didn't matter how I felt about him, or *why* I felt anything for him anymore.

I forced a smile and got out of my car, zipping up my coat as I examined everything he was holding in addition to his backpack: a long, black contraption and what appeared to be a camera bag hanging from his forearm. "Do you want some help?" I offered.

"Naw, I've got it," he smiled. He watched me approach, his eyes admiring me. "You look really nice tonight, May."

I looked down at my clothing. Nothing unusual; jeans, tennis shoes, my coat. He could tell by the shake of my head that I was denying his claim. "You always look nice," he clarified, tilting my chin up with his fingertip to look into my eyes.

He was crowding me, but not in a bad way. I never felt safer than when I was with him. I marveled at the look in his eyes, inwardly cursing myself because I had a secret I knew would ruin everything. I rubbed my lips together, trying to keep him from seeing just how torn I was apart inside. "Thank you. Where are we going?"

"Down the path to one of the lookout points." He led the way and peered sideways at me. "You alright?"

"I'm good. It's just been a long day." I could tell he didn't really believe me. In just a couple short weeks, I was already catching on to Alex's subtle cues and expressions. But I knew I wasn't ready to tell him the truth. Even if I could just forget about it for an hour or two, I knew I would be able to gather the courage to do so. It was inevitable, and he deserved to know. "So what is this stuff?"

"Ever heard of astrophotography?" he asked, the bags swaying as we went down the steepest curve of the path. We came to a bench and he shrugged everything off onto the concrete surface.

"I haven't. But I'm assuming it has something to do with astronomy and photography?"

"Very good," he winked at me. "My mom dabbled in portrait photography, but her true love was astrophotography. This is all of her stuff."

I watched as he unzipped the camera bag. In it were an enormous digital camera and a couple different lenses. "Fancy," I said as he began assembling what he needed.

"I'm not nearly as good at this as she was, but I'm learning."

"So you took up riding for your dad, and photography and music for your mom?"

He stood up straight and nodded at me. "Yeah. I guess I just didn't want their passions to disappear." He picked up the metal contraption and unfolded it, and I soon realized it was a tripod. He was quiet as he attached the camera to it.

I didn't deserve to be here. Alex was letting me see this side of him: the side I couldn't have imagined him showing anyone else unless he trusted them. It felt like he was giving me a gift I wasn't worthy of. I took my eyes off him and sat down on the bench because my head was spinning. Sighing, I stared at the starry canopy he would be photographing. "You know, I honestly can't think of a single hobby that my mom has ever enjoyed." I looked at him again. "That's pretty sad, isn't it?"

He frowned. "It is. Is she a workaholic?"

"Very much so."

Alex bent and looked through the viewfinder, pressing a button on a remote that was attached to the camera. The shutter clicked. He did this a few more times before changing some settings, and then he came to sit with me. "It's on a timed exposure now," he explained. "We'll get some streaks from the stars. I'll show you how it all works in a bit."

"I bet it'll be beautiful," I whispered.

He nodded, resting his elbows on his knees. "I've always loved sitting out in the open at night, making out shapes in the stars. I couldn't tell you what all of the constellations are though, and I'm pretty sure I've made most of them up . . ." he laughed. "But it's always given me a feeling of peace. Especially these last two years."

The breeze was cold and salty. I could hear the waves crashing, but I could only make out their silvery caps in the moonlight. The grass around us swayed. This place really should have given me peace. I was only thankful that Alex couldn't really see my face.

I didn't say anything, scared my voice would betray me. I wanted him to keep talking. Just the tone of his voice was soothing.

But he didn't speak. He was content to sit with me. I wished I could say the same.

What would he say if he knew the truth? We hadn't even discussed what this thing between us *was*. Was it anything? Did Alex see the kisses we had shared as something fleeting? How did *I* see them?

I stared down at my wringing hands. I could feel my pulse in my temples. I was exhausted, as if I had the flu, except I knew I didn't. I had something much more life-altering.

There was no easy answer. If I told him, it would be in the open. He knew everything else, so why not this? If I didn't tell him, he would find out eventually . . . unless I opted to terminate my pregnancy anyway.

The thing was, I didn't even know if I was pro-choice. My viewpoint had shifted throughout my life, back and forth, back and forth. I had never really known how to feel about it. Something inside of me had always felt resistant to the idea of abortion though.

But I had never imagined I would be the one facing this decision. Had I actually been naive enough to think this sort of thing could never happen to me?

I didn't know what to do. I didn't know what to feel. It was on the tip of my tongue; all I had to do was say it. For the first time, I actually wished Alex could read my mind. I wished he was in tune enough to know that something was horribly wrong. But perhaps he was, and he knew if I trusted him, I would let him in.

I did trust him.

"I'm pregnant," I breathed, barely above a whisper. The words were so quiet and matter-of-fact that Alex actually looked at me with confusion clearly etched on his face. I watched him process what I said, his face shrouded by shadows, but his eyes clearly visible. It was like an internal conversation was flickering behind his eyes.

I don't know what I had expected. Was it for him to offer some kind of wisdom? Was it for him to stay? To abandon me on this bench? His silence was unnerving. For the first time, he was speechless.

"Well. Now you know." I stood up and tucked my hands into my coat. "I should get going. Thanks for inviting me out, but I think I should head home. I have homework." *Things I can barely manage when I'm not carrying my rapist's baby,* I thought, turning toward the path.

"May, wait. I'm sorry I didn't say anything. I was just—"

"Surprised?" I answered, facing him. "Confused? Unsure of what to say to the girl you kissed just yesterday? I get it, Alex. I don't expect anything from you. I'm just realizing how crazy this was; how delusional I must be."

"What do you mean?" he shook his head. "You're not delusional, May. I care for you."

"That's not what I mean. I mean that you're great. You're amazing, even. And me? I'm ruined, Alex. You have enough pain. You don't need mine."

"I don't see it that way."

"Well, I do," I promised vehemently. "And now I'm not only ruined, but I'm pregnant. No matter how many times I say it, or think it, it doesn't make any more sense than that. Had I actually thought I could entertain some sort of relationship with you? Two *weeks* after being assaulted?" I paused, grinding my teeth together. "I'm such an idiot." I turned away and began scaling the steep concrete slope.

"You're not ruined. I'm not ruined. That's what I'm trying to show you."

I kept walking, and I didn't stop until I was heaving for air by my car. Sweat trickled down my forehead as I climbed inside. Laying my hands on my abdomen, I bent forward and caught my breath.

When I sat up straight a while later, I startled, noticing someone in the corner of my eye. I immediately realized it was Alex. He was standing at the path entrance, staring out at the ocean, his back to me.

He was letting me leave, but he was making sure I made it safely. That is what almost caused me to flee from my car and beg him to hold me and take this all away. Instead, I used what little resolve I had left to start the engine and back out of the parking lot.

Twenty-One

THERE WERE TWO THINGS I learned that night. First: in the state of Oregon, a minor could have an abortion without the permission of a parent. Second: I learned I was capable of truly considering such a means to an end.

I don't know how long I sat at my computer in my bedroom in the dark, the light from the monitor drowning out my surroundings. All I could do was stare at the logo for a local abortion clinic, wondering what it would be like if I chose this option. Their slogan was "Helping women reclaim their future." It seemed like such a fallacy because I hadn't even considered my future since the day all of this was thrust upon me. I hadn't even realized how much I had given up until then, sitting there with the pink emblem burning itself into my mind.

I wondered if aborting my body's unwanted inhabitant would change anything. I already felt hopeless. Lost. Damaged. Already I despised what had taken root inside of me. I despised it as much as I despised its father.

Its father. That title didn't even seem to fit, and Tyler wasn't deserving of it. I knew I was certainly not a mother; I was merely a facilitator.

I looked down at my abdomen and my lips began to quiver. *How dare he,* I thought. *How dare he put this inside of me? How dare he take what wasn't his?*

I wept, rocking back and forth, hating him; hating his fetus. Hating *myself*. "I want it gone," I cried quietly, hoping my groans wouldn't be heard down the hall.

My phone dinged. Its light swirled and flickered into my watery eyes. Sniffing loudly, I blinked a few times and listened to the voicemail:

"I know you need time and space," Alex said gently. "I will give you that. I just wanted you to know I'm here if you ever want to talk."

I put my phone down and dragged myself to bed.

* * *

"Stop moving!"

My head whipped to the side to escape his lips, trying to bring my legs together as he blocked my attempt with his body. "Please stop," I begged, feeling him struggle to remove my underwear. He couldn't take them off while he was between my legs, so he tore the fabric apart.

"I'll be quick," he said, as if it excused what he was doing.

The pain was searing. One moment I was sobbing and the next I couldn't even breathe. "Please," I whispered, burying my face into the plush pillows on Tyler's bed, willing myself to dissolve into it.

"May."

Hands shook me. My eyes snapped open and I saw my mom standing over me, her brows pulled together. "Do you want to tell me what this is?" she asked, holding my phone in front of my face. I blinked over and over, trying to adjust my vision. On the screen was a text from Addison.

> Addison: Hey. My mom found the pregnancy test in my trash can. I didn't tell her it was yours, but she guessed it. She said she sensed something was up with you. I'm so sorry, May. I should have remembered to get rid of it.

I sat up slowly and forced myself to look at her. For once, I couldn't tell what she was thinking. I had never seen her look so pale and angry and confused. "Why were you looking through my phone?" was all I could ask, but I knew immediately that it was the wrong thing to say.

"Your phone lit up when I was taking your laundry basket," she said through her teeth. "I'm not going to ask you to explain again."

I felt myself deflate. I wished I could disappear. "What is there to explain?" I murmured hopelessly. "You already know."

She stared at me, her lips a razor-thin line. "You couldn't have thought to use protection? Or tell me you wanted to be on the pill? What have you honestly learned about responsibility, May? You are not the daughter I raised."

She might as well have stabbed me in the gut. I hugged my waist and tried not to let her see me cry. "The condom broke," I said. It had to be true. Tyler wore a condom, yet clearly it had failed. I couldn't let her know the rest of the story because if I did, I would never have a hope of moving on from this and not dragging it out in a legal case.

Just knowing there had been a condom involved seemed to quench at least a little bit of the fire fueling her anger. She exhaled loudly, her shoulders sagging. "Who is the father?"

Oh, God. Please don't ask me this. I shook my head, wishing this was just an extension of the dream she had shaken me from. I knew if I told her who he was, she would insist on talking to him. I couldn't let that happen. No matter what, she would seek him out. "I was stupid, okay? I drank at that party I went to a couple weeks ago. I slept with a cousin of one of the girls who was invited from a different school. I don't remember his name." She already thought I was a disappointment anyway, so what did I have to lose in lying about a one-night stand?

I was amazed that even to me, it didn't sound like I was lying. The explanation had tumbled from my mouth with such ease that even I almost believed it. In this case, lying was becoming much, much easier than the truth.

"Since when do you drink? And since when would you sleep with some random guy you just met?" she seethed, standing up to pace by my bed. "I can't believe you would do this!"

Her hateful tone cut me to the bone. If only she knew *I was a victim*. All I could do was take her scathing fury and pretend like it was justified. "I know it was stupid, alright?" I spat, throwing the blankets off to get to my feet. "But you don't have to worry about it. I'm taking care of it soon. I know I'm not ready to be a mother." *To any child, and especially this one.*

She paused and crossed her arms. "That's the smartest thing you've said in a while," she stated with control over every syllable. "Get dressed. You still have responsibilities."

And I did get dressed, but I didn't make it downstairs until it was well past the time for class to start. Instead, I lay in a ball on the bathroom floor on the plush, purple carpet beneath me as I sobbed.

For the first time in my entire life, I wished my life could end.

Now

I WAS IN LABOR for fifteen hours with my daughter. After two failed attempts at an epidural, I dilated to ten centimeters in a matter of thirty minutes. I thought she was going to split me in two, and I'm pretty sure I deafened everyone in the room with my screams. But about halfway through pushing efforts, I had a moment where I drew on my inner strength. I had to be strong. I couldn't be weak any longer. My daughter needed me.

I was silent and determined until she entered the world. She was wailing and screeching in disapproval of her cold, sudden arrival. The moment I saw her, I cried in longing. I needed to hold her. I needed to see her face.

And I know I'm not as strong as I was in those fleeting minutes. Sometimes I think I'm just as weak as I was before. But it's moments like these, when she takes my cheeks between her hands and makes her lips vibrate together, drooling bubbles around her enormous grin that I feel like I can go on. She is my lifeline.

Then

"WELL, YOU'RE CLEARLY going to miss school today. I think we should go ahead and tell your father, don't you think?"

I stopped in my tracks and dropped my book bag on the floor next to the kitchen island. "I really should go to class . . . ."

"You should," she responded sharply. "But you won't. I will call the school to notify them of your absence and then arrange a meeting time with your father. I'll wait for you in the car."

The door slammed behind her. I pushed my hands into my hair and closed my eyes.

"You're having a baby?" Grace asked behind me.

I shook my head. "No. I don't think I am."

She clearly understood what I meant. Her lips trembled. "I hope you'll change your mind. It's innocent, you know?"

I realized then that Grace might not have been a carbon copy of our mother. And had she said anything else, anything at all, I wouldn't have loathed this sign of independence. "It's none of your business, Grace," I said flatly, and made my way out the door.

* * *

MY INSIDES FELT HOLLOW as my mom and I sat on the other side of my father's desk, watching him rifle through charts with his glasses hanging low on the bridge of his nose. "Did you get in trouble at school or something?" he asked, obviously buried with work, which only made me feel guilty for burdening him with something such as this in the middle of his shift.

"Stop and listen for a moment, Lucas. For God's sake!"

I looked at Mom, cringing. Her nostrils were flaring with each breath and she was red in the face. The sound of papers moving around ceased and I turned my head to find my father watching me. We finally had his attention and I was terrified.

"What is it, May?" he asked, taking his glasses off.

I watched him fold them and set them aside, inhaling a deep breath to muster up the courage to speak. My hand went to my stomach. "Dad, I . . ." I cleared my throat when my voice cracked. "I'm—"

"Dr. O'Hara, we have a rape victim. She has trauma to the back of her skull."

My breath left me in a rush of shock and defeat.

He looked at the nurse in his doorway. "I'm busy, Andrea. Page Dr. Shrader."

"Dr. Shrader is in the O.R. There's nobody else."

He sighed and nodded, putting his glasses back on. "Wait here, May. I'll be as quick as I can."

"Sit your ass back down!" Mom snapped. "Give your daughter five minutes to talk."

"Dr. O'Hara?" the nurse inquired, casting my mom a glare.

"The girl may not have five minutes." He headed for the door.

"Lucas, May is pregnant."

I whipped around to face her, my mouth dropping open in humiliation. I heard Andrea's shoes hit the tile as she sprinted away, and the door closed behind her. Slowly I turned to find my father staring down at me. His hand clutched the doorknob. "What did your mother just say?"

I rose to my feet, looking up at him in utter shame. "It's true. I'm sorry, Dad. I didn't mean—"

What? I didn't mean to get raped? I didn't mean to lie and say it was with someone else? That it was consensual?

"I'm sorry to let you down."

He adjusted his stethoscope around his neck, his jaw flexing rhythmically. "We will discuss this further tonight."

And then he was gone.

Twenty-Two

WE ALL SAT AROUND the kitchen table, Grace included, since my mom had insisted this was her business too. I kept my eyes on the planks that made up the surface, examining the grain of the wood as if it were of great interest. Nobody had said anything yet. And I didn't know what they wanted to hear.

"Have you considered the alternative?" Mom asked.

I looked at her blankly. "What alternative?"

"Keeping it," Dad said.

I swallowed, shifting in my seat. I was surprised it was even an option they would consider viable. "No. I haven't."

"What does the father think?"

I turned my eyes to my dad, exhaling slowly to calm my heartbeat. "He doesn't know. I don't even know how to contact him."

"You can't be serious," he sighed in disbelief.

"Well, I don't think it's something you should consider," Mom said, getting my attention. "You're only seventeen. You have college and a career ahead of you." She fingered the doily in front of her. "Wouldn't you agree, Lucas?"

"I think it's her decision and we should be supportive either way."

Mom rolled her eyes. "I think it's obvious what she wants."

"Do you know when you conceived?" Dad asked, ignoring her.

I exhaled slowly, trying to keep my emotions under control. "About two and a half weeks ago? We only had . . ." I straightened in my chair. "It was only one time."

Dad nodded. "When was your period due?" he asked, his tone as clinical as if he were speaking to one of his patients.

I pushed my hands into my hair, staring straight down at the table. "A couple days ago."

"You're very early," he sighed. "So there's time to decide. I'm not a proponent of abortion as a form of birth control, and had this been rape, I would feel differently. But you made your bed, May. Only you can decide whether or not to sleep in it."

My hands trembled. I was so close to telling them it *was* rape, just so that their false judgment would cease. But then everyone else would judge me. The shame was too crippling. All I could do was sit there, frozen under the stares I could feel, even from Grace, who hadn't said a word. "Can I go to my room?" I whispered.

"We're not done yet," Dad said. "You may or may not abort this pregnancy, but until you decide, you need to be educated on prenatal care."

For the next half hour I was drowned in information about prenatal vitamins, proper nutrition, medications I could no longer take, and what to expect in my body. The whole speech was torture, mainly because my dad was the last person I wanted to hear it from — especially the parts about cervical mucus and changes in my breasts. Somewhere along the way I begged to just wait and hear this from the doctor who would be performing my exam, and he finally relented. Though, I was abundantly aware of how big of a disappointment I was.

It was all pointless anyway. Staying pregnant was simply not an option.

* * *

ADDISON WAS WAITING for me by my locker the next morning. Her tired eyes widened when she saw me coming. "I've been so worried about you. I'm so sorry, May. I shouldn't have been so careless."

"It's alright. Really," I assured her as I turned the dial. "It actually turned out alright. They're pissed, really pissed, but at least I don't have to try to hide it from them."

"So you told them everything?"

I paused to look at her. "No. Not everything. But I don't think they'll be asking who the father is anymore."

"How did you manage that?"

"I told them it was a one night stand," I shrugged. "Which made them even more pissed. It doesn't matter though. I'm having an exam tonight and a consult to learn what I can do to fix this."

Addison nodded slowly. It was obvious she wanted to say something. "What is it?" I asked.

"It's just . . . I hope you'll take some time to think about whether or not you really want to do this."

"Look, I know you're against abortion," I whispered so only she would hear. "But I—"

"It doesn't matter what I'm for or against, May. I can't tell you what to do in this situation. I just want you to acknowledge there might be some repercussions."

"What kind of repercussions would there be if I *don't* do it?" I retorted. "I can list a few, the first being a baby."

She shook her head. "Girls who have abortions are more likely to struggle with suicidal thoughts. Lots of them dream about their infant for years to come."

Anger simmered in my veins. "This isn't a convenience thing. There's no way in hell I'll regret this, and you know it." I sighed heavily. "Everyone has an opinion regarding what I should do with this . . . *intruder* in my body. But nothing could be worse than having to look at its face and see Tyler for the rest of my life." At that moment, I saw him coming up the hall with his throng of followers. We met eyes briefly and I was the first to look away.

"How can you even be in the same school with him?" Addison asked. "You already have to see his face."

"I don't have a choice. And he hasn't said a word to me except to apologize, so I can at least avoid him most of the time."

"Look," Addison said, tucking a loose wisp of hair behind her ear. "I love you, May. You're my best friend. That's why I feel like I need to be honest with you and help you make an informed decision. What kind of friend would I be if I said nothing and blindly supported a choice that could affect you in a way you might never expect?"

My anger dissolved a little. "I know you're looking out for me. And I promise I'll think about it. But I need to know something. Will you support me if I still choose my way?"

She pulled me into a hug. "You know I will."

I squeezed her. "I can't believe I'm even in this position," I whispered. "This all feels like just some nightmare I'll wake up from if I try hard enough. When will I wake up?"

She let go of me but took my hands. "Have you ever had a nightmare that was so awful you knew you were dreaming? And somehow you managed to make yourself dream about something else?"

"Once or twice," I nodded.

"You can't wake up from this one, but maybe you can find your way into a new dream."

Her wisdom gave me hope. I drew on her strength. "I'll try."

* * *

THE SKY HAD OPENED UP on the way to the abortion clinic. Mom parked in one of the few spaces allotted for patients. I stared at the building beyond the windshield wipers that beat back and forth; back and forth. I was just about to unbuckle my seatbelt when she started talking.

"You were a surprise. Your father and I hadn't even planned on having children."

I looked at her, confused. She continued, staring at something in the distance. "When I was pregnant with you, I had all of these expectations. I thought motherhood would be a breeze: I would come home from work, pay the nanny, and spend the rest of the evening bonding with you. I thought you would be a heavy sleeper like your father, and quiet and reserved like me." A dreamy smile came to her lips and she shook her head. "You screamed *constantly*. When we took you home from the hospital, you didn't stop crying for six months. There was one night I lost an important court case and you were wailing, and I was so stressed I began to cry myself, and I asked your father what I was doing so terribly wrong that I couldn't comfort you."

I wondered why she was telling me this. She wiped the corner of her eye with her fingertip and when she spoke again, she was struggling for control. "But you know, he could pick you up and instantly you would calm down. I had been telling myself that you were just a difficult baby; that it was a phase you would grow out of. But I realized I just didn't have it. I didn't have mothering capabilities, nor the instinct to give you what you needed." She looked at me and a mascara-tinged tear slipped down her cheek. "But as ill-prepared as I was, and as horrible I was at all of this, it didn't change how much I loved you. I don't show it nearly enough. Sometimes I don't think I know how. But I fell in love for the first time when I saw you. And I have watched you grow into an independent, bold, compassionate, fiery young woman that I am so proud of. Please forgive me for withholding how I've truly seen you throughout these years. Forgive me for resenting the fact that I wasn't enough. I just wanted to be enough."

I reached out to her and hugged her tightly, resting my cheek on her shoulder while we both cried together for the first time since I was a baby. "I forgive you."

She combed her fingers through my hair and exhaled like she was letting go of that guilt. "Even though you've made a mistake, I'm still proud of you." We looked at each other when I sat back. "I don't want to see you choose a life that will be more difficult than you are prepared for. But I want you to know that if you choose to keep this child, you will have your father's and my blessing."

I nodded, but I was more confused than ever about the path I should take. What if I *didn't* see Tyler's face when I looked at my child? What if it could be a blessing in disguise? What if there was more to this than I thought?

Two weeks. Only two weeks and a few days had passed, and so much had changed. My innocence had been taken from me. I had almost given my heart to someone who I thought might be able to fix me. I had possibly broken his in my selfishness. And now I was pregnant. I wondered what else could possibly add to this invisible burden I felt pressing me into the ground.

"Let's go," she said. We dashed through the rain under a single umbrella.

Twenty-Three

MOM CLOSED THE UMBRELLA after we stepped through the glass door of the clinic. I looked around the room and noticed there was only one other patient: a woman sitting in a chair in the corner, blotting her face with a crumpled up tissue. I wondered if she had been raped too. The air felt sterile but musty, as if the carpet was holding onto dust and moisture. My heart thumped unevenly as I approached the desk, greeted by an older woman with a stylish black bob. "Good afternoon," she smiled, setting her cup of coffee aside. "Can I help you?"

I looked at my mom, expecting her to inform the receptionist of why we were here, but she only gave me an encouraging nod to speak for myself. I met eyes with the woman and forced the words out. "I want to talk to someone about an abortion?" I said, but it sounded like a question; I wasn't even sure if that was what I wanted, even though I knew how badly I wanted this to be over with.

"Alright. Our clinic requires a pre-abortion consult before you schedule an actual appointment. Please collect your urine in this cup and we will confirm pregnancy while you fill out your medical history. What is your name?"

I cleared my throat. "May O'Hara."

She nodded and scribbled on the side of a plastic cup with a blue lid. After setting it in front of me, she pointed to the bathroom around the corner. "There's a little door in the bathroom. When you're finished, set the cup on the shelf behind it and we will take it from there."

I took the cup and tapped my finger on it while I made my way to the bathroom. The woman in the corner looked up at me and offered a sad smile, which I couldn't return. I closed the door, exhaling a breath I had been holding as I looked at myself in the mirror.

My eyes were sunken in and dull. I was pale and thin. What had happened to me? Where had I gone? *Stop moving!* Tyler shouted in my mind. My face stung where he hit me. I touched my cheek, tracing the area that still hurt, but not from an actual bruise. I wondered if it would always hurt. I wondered if I would ever stop hearing him in my mind; feeling him invading my innocence. I tore myself away from the mirror and did what the nurse had asked. Before I left, I scrubbed my face with the icy water that refused to turn warm. I rested my palms on the porcelain sink and watched the water drip off of my face, taking a few deep breaths to calm my nerves.

Mom was waiting for me with the clipboard in her lap. I sat next to her and took it, seeing she had already filled in my personal information. "Thank you," I mumbled, working through the checklist. They really wanted to know *everything*—everything down to my sexual activity, my exposure to STDs, what my symptoms were, and a dozen other gruesome things I couldn't believe I was reading. I felt my mother watching me as I filled it out, my cheeks burning red hot because I might as well have been telling her all of it for myself.

Luckily, there wasn't much to tell. I had only had sex one time.

I finished filling out the final questions just as my name was called by a nurse in pink scrubs. I stood and brought the clipboard to her, then followed her with my mother down a hallway with at least a dozen doors on each side. She hadn't even greeted me. She looked at me like I was just another face with the same story. "Come on in. I'm Lacy," she said when we reached a door at the end of the hall. "Have a seat."

We sat. On the walls were medical diagrams of a woman's anatomy, along with a couple inspirational posters that said things like "Nobody can walk in your shoes but you," and "We are pro-life: *your* life."

"I understand you are considering an abortion, May?"

"I am," I answered meekly.

"Looks like your period was due a few days ago, so that puts you at about four weeks. Would you like me to educate you about the options you have?"

I nodded.

"At this point, you have two options. You can either have a medical abortion, which is the non-surgical type of abortion. You would be given an abortifacient medication and your body would go through the process on its own. Your other option would be a surgical abortion. With this option, the fetus and placenta are removed from the uterus with the use of a few simple instruments. You would be awake and the actual procedure only takes about five to ten minutes. Our clinic offers this option as early as four weeks."

I was trembling. It all sounded so complicated and traumatic. "Do they hurt? Both ways?"

She laced her fingers together on the desk and nodded. "With the medication, you would experience intense cramping and moderate to heavy bleeding. Some women say it is no worse than a bad period though. It takes a couple days. With the surgical option, you would only experience minor discomfort throughout the procedure."

"I want that one then," I said without even having to think about it. "I don't want to be in pain for days. I just want this over with."

"I understand. Would you like me to explain the procedure to you in detail so that you know what to expect?"

"No," I shook my head. "I don't want to know about it. I just want it done."

She smiled stiffly. "Let me rephrase: I am required to educate you, at least on the basics, so that you can make an informed decision."

"And to cover your asses," Mom interjected.

The woman didn't even glance at her. "If at any point what I am saying makes you uncomfortable, please let me know."

"Alright," I relented.

"When you arrive for your appointment, the doctor will review your medical history and perform an ultrasound to confirm your pregnancy's gestation. You will not have to see the ultrasound images if you don't want to. Then you will be given some medication:

Ibuprofen, Vicodin, and Valium. These will help with swelling, pain, and anxiety. You will be left alone for a while to let the medications take effect, and then the procedure will begin. During the procedure, the doctor will insert a speculum into your vagina. You will then be cleaned, and your cervix will be numbed with a local anesthetic. The doctor will dilate you, and then he will insert a small tube into your uterus to perform the suction abortion."

I was nauseous. My head spun wildly, making me close my eyes. "And then what?"

"Then you'll be done. You will be sent home to rest and you can resume normal activities the following day. You will have some bleeding, but no heavier than a normal period."

"And the emotional side of things?" Mom asked. "How is she going to feel about this later?"

"Let me assure you—women all around the world go on to lead normal lives after an abortion. Very few ever regret their decision. But this is why we like to meet with our patients prior to their appointment. We want them to have all the tools necessary to choose what's best for them. I can also recommend some excellent support groups and counseling resources if her recovery proves to be difficult."

"It's already difficult," I said. "An abortion won't change that. So schedule me please. I want this done as soon as possible."

"Very well," the nurse nodded. She turned to her computer and typed a few things. "Would a weekend be best for you?"

"Of course. She has school," Mom said.

Lacy seemed annoyed that my mother was answering for me. "A Saturday please," I clarified.

"I can get you in this Saturday at 9AM."

"Good," I said.

"Don't eat or drink anything the morning of your appointment. Make sure you don't consume any alcohol or Aspirin. Dress comfortably. Will you be driving her, ma'am?"

Mom nodded. "Yes."

Lacy slid a business card to me with the doctor's name and my appointment time scribbled on it. "We will see you then. Please don't hesitate to call if you have any questions. And if you are at all hesitant over the next few days, we can make you another appointment with one of our counselors."

"Thank you," I murmured and stood with my mother. We exited down the hallway, and the last thing I heard before stepping into the waiting area was a woman groaning in pain behind a closed door.

That sound followed me to the car and tormented me throughout the duration of our drive home.

Twenty-Four

IT WAS 6PM WHEN WE PULLED into our driveway. I didn't want to be there. We had been silent during the drive and with each passing second, I found myself longing to be alone. I needed to think, and that wasn't going to happen at my house. "Mom, is it alright if I go to the barn? I only have one assignment tonight and I'm already halfway done with it."

"Sure. I think that'd be alright. Do you want to take Grace?"

I shook my head. "I just need to be alone. I need to think about everything."

"Alright," she said, turning off the ignition. "Just try to be home by eight. I'll keep dinner warm for you."

Since when did Mom cook? I could sense a shift in her demeanor today. I wondered if she blamed herself for my getting pregnant. "Thanks. And I will."

I got out of the car and took my backpack to my Jeep.

* * *

I WAS THE ONLY ONE at the stable when I arrived. It was actually comforting to think that nobody would want to venture out in this weather but me. Cash was eating the last remnants of his grain when I came to his stall. He saw me and his ears flicked forward, and he left behind the last few pellets to come and see me. "Hey," I smiled softly and detangled his forelock with my fingers. I braided it between his eyes. "Sorry I haven't been around." I sighed. "Let's ride in the indoor arena today."

I didn't move away from his stall for his halter though. Instead I stared at his enormous, soft brown eyes as they blinked lazily from my touch. My throat tightened. "What am I supposed to do, boy?" I whispered, resting my forehead on his. Tears fell onto his fur. I wondered if there would ever come a day when I wouldn't cry. "Why did this have to happen? I hate him. I hate him so much."

I opened the door and went inside to hug his neck. I buried my face against his shoulder and let myself fall apart. He stood quietly, unmoving. Somehow I knew he was comforting me. I could feel it. I folded my arms on his back and sobbed into the crook of my elbow, wanting to get it all out here and now. I never wanted to feel this broken again.

Someone touched my shoulder. I gasped and lifted my head, seeing Alex standing behind me. We looked at each other for a moment before he stepped forward and wrapped his arms around me. "It's okay," he whispered by my ear. "I've got you."

I hesitated at first, but I slowly slid my arms around his waist and clung to him, swallowed in his safe and warm embrace. "What are you doing here?" I asked. The question sounded angry, but it wasn't. Had he known I needed him?

"I needed to clear my head. This is where I come to do that."

I almost laughed as I let go of him. "Me too," I said, wiping my face with the sleeve of my hoodie. He looked sad. His eyes were red and swollen. I hoped I hadn't done this to him, yet I couldn't believe I was presumptuous enough to think he would be this distraught over the things I said. "Do you want to talk about it?" I asked. I didn't have anything to offer him other than a listening ear, and I definitely didn't want to talk about my own situation.

He shrugged and stroked Cash's jaw. "It's the anniversary of my parents' death today," he said. His voice was course and gravelly. "Officially two years. It just hit me hard, I guess. But I'm alright." He smiled, but it was the first time Alex had ever smiled that it didn't look genuine.

"It's okay if you're not," I assured him. I wished I had something wise to say; some eloquent encouragement to offer that would bring a little bit of light to him on this dark day. "Alex, I'm really sorry about the things I said to you the other day. I put words in your mouth and made assumptions that weren't fair. You've been such a good friend to me over these last couple of weeks."

"You don't have to apologize," he insisted. "I can't possibly know what this is like for you, but I understood why you pushed me away."

I wondered how I could have been so selfish. "No, I do have to apologize. I'm not the only one who's hurting. It's like we crossed paths at our lowest points. Your presence in my life confused me because my trust in people has been shaken. Everything I thought I knew about my life has been twisted and torn until I don't even recognize myself anymore. And you have been so good to me. I think I thought you could fix me." My eyes flooded. "I'm sorry. If you can forgive me, I promise to be a good friend to you."

"There's nothing to forgive," he said softly. The pain was gone from his face as he looked into my eyes, seeming to want to say more. He was quiet and thoughtful. Accepting. He patted Cash's neck and turned those sparkling blues on me again. "And I would love your friendship. I think we can help each other be strong. I just hope you know that you're strong on your own, May. You don't need anyone to fix you."

"Maybe not," I agreed. "It's just . . . today I'm wondering if I'll ever be the way I was before all of this happened." I paused, watching him. "Do you ever feel that way?"

He smiled sadly. "All the time. But I think once you've experienced loss and devastation, you can't ever go back. You just have to go forward."

"How are you doing it?"

"Well, it hasn't been a smooth transition. I went from being a big city music major to a bookstore owner in a town I never imagined myself living in. And I'm thankful, because in a way it's allowed me to discover deeper parts of myself. I'm learning I'm stronger than I thought; that I can figure all of this out without guidance from family. I guess it's taught me there is so much more to life than I originally thought. I actually resented this town when I first moved here."

"You don't anymore?"

"No. I'm learning to love walking down by the boat docks in the early morning, hearing nothing but gulls and a small town waking up. I'm learning to look at each day like something to embrace and appreciate. I'm not the person I was a couple years ago, or even a couple months ago. I used to think all there was to life was music and enormous ambitions. I'd like to think I still have those ambitions, and of course I still have music, but that's not all there is. And I know I could never understand what you're going through, but I think the same might be true for you. You might not ever feel like the person you were a few weeks ago, but maybe you can grow into someone who will nod at the past with appreciation for what it was, and accept new possibilities."

I realized that Alex was a lot like Addison. That was perhaps why I felt so safe with him. And he was so wise; much wiser than me. "I can't imagine that now, but I hope you're right. Do you think we would have been good friends if we had met a couple years ago?"

He smiled. "I think we would have been good friends. But I think we met at just the right time."

"Yeah," I smiled too. "I think you're right."

His eyes grew serious. "How are you feeling?"

I knew he was referring to my pregnancy. I tucked my hands into my hoodie and flattened my palm against my abdomen. "Confused. Scared. Lost." I shook my head. "I had an appointment tonight at Newport Women's Clinic."

"An ultrasound?"

"No. Just a consult. I, um . . . I have an appointment for Saturday. I think I'm going to terminate." I said the last part with very little emotion and braced for his response.

He looked down at the ground and nodded slowly. He seemed to struggle with how to respond. I spared him from needing to think of something to say. "I don't know how that makes you feel. My friend Addison has tried to talk me out of it. My sister feels that way too. But it's the only option for me. I don't think I would choose this if had gotten pregnant under different circumstances."

He looked at me again, still nodding. "Nobody can tell you what to do, May. I could never possibly know how you're feeling, and it's not my job to influence you one way or the other."

"How do you feel about it? About abortion?" I asked.

He ran his hand over Cash's neck, pursing his lips thoughtfully. "I was raised to believe that life begins at conception. It was my parents' moral conviction, and I suppose it's always been mine too."

I chewed on my lip. Even though I knew what he said wouldn't influence me, I still cared what he thought. "So you feel like it's wrong, even in my case?"

He looked at me. "The thought of it grieves me in a lot of ways. I've grieved for you, that you even have to consider doing this. And I've grieved for the baby."

The word "baby" made me tense up. I had refused to even acknowledge that word. That word made what I was planning to do seem so barbaric and inhuman. "I don't even know how I would make it through this pregnancy. I can't explain to you how invaded my body feels right now."

"I know," he said gently. "And that's why I can't tell you what to do. I *hope* you'll consider there might be a way to make this awful thing that happened to you into a good thing."

"How is that even possible?" I sighed, frustrated.

"I don't know," he shook his head. "Adoption, maybe? For a couple who can't have kids?"

"So I would grow this child inside of me, potentially become somewhat attached, and then have to give it away? Alex, enough has already been stolen from me. Maybe this makes me an awful person, but—"

"This doesn't make you awful," he insisted. "It makes you human. You're trying to do the right thing for yourself."

But what if he was right? What if it was my responsibility to care about the life that was growing inside of me, even if it hadn't been wanted? I was so confused.

"Whatever you choose, it won't change how I see you. But I think this choice is so much deeper than you realize right now."

"What do you mean?" I sighed hopelessly.

"It isn't about whether or not you should have this baby," he said, looking into my eyes. "It's about how you're going to choose to live your life beyond this. It's about what you're going to do with what happened to you."

I knew Alex couldn't possible understand what it was like to be raped; what it was like to bear that rapist's child. But he understood what losing your identity felt like. "Do you remember that question I asked you? About being a bird or a fish?" I asked.

"Yes," he nodded.

My stomach tightened into a knot. "He asked me that question before he . . ." I took a deep breath. "Anyway, I told him I identified more as a bird than a fish."

Alex's jaw flexed. "And then he tried to break you."

"Yeah." I blinked back tears, but they still fell.

He reached out and took my hand. "Don't let him, May."

"But that's just it. I'm afraid he already did."

Alex smiled and shook his head, lifting his hand to touch my cheek in the exact spot that Tyler had hit me. His touch was warm and soothing, and I leaned into it so that maybe, just maybe it would be the touch I would remember forever. "I don't see a girl who is broken. Bruised, maybe. But not broken," he said softly.

"Do you really think so?"

"I know so. Now what do you say we go ride?"

I breathed out slowly. "I'd say that sounds amazing."

We rode together until my mom called to inform me that it was getting too late. By the time I had put Cash up for the night, I was actually genuinely laughing. Alex hugged me before I left. I knew that spark was still there. In fact, it was easier to distinguish this time. But if anything was ever to happen between us, it would have to wait.

Twenty-Five

I WAS TOO SICK to go to school the next day. And the day after that. It honestly felt like I was dying; like my body was giving up from the stress and sickness. And the worst part of it was that I couldn't even be happy about it. Most women who want a baby are more than happy to endure a little morning sickness. I just felt cursed.

Addison and Danika came to check on me both days after school. By the afternoon I was feeling well enough to at least get out of bed, so I was able to talk to them for a while. They tried to keep it light. I could still sense a wall around Danika, and I actually felt guilty that she might still be blaming herself.

Alex called on Thursday after my friends had gone home for the night. After learning how sick I was, he offered to bring some ginger ale and a cheesy movie to watch. I was about to refuse because it was one thing to let your girlfriends see you looking like the walking dead; it was another for a guy you just kissed a week ago to see the same thing. But in the end, his offer to watch *The Princess Bride* won me over. I hadn't seen it since I was a kid, and I missed him.

I came downstairs after showering and was surprised to stumble upon Alex sitting in the kitchen, talking to my parents. I hadn't expected him so early. "Hey," he grinned. "I come bearing gifts."

I laughed uncomfortably, toweling the ends of my hair as I approached. At least I had opted for pajamas instead of a bathrobe.

He lifted what looked like a beer bottle, but I quickly realized it was some kind of organic ginger ale. "Fancy," I smirked.

"Says it has real, fresh ginger," he said, reading the bottle. "And, of course . . ." He pulled a package of saltines out of his coat pocket, offering them both to me with a smile.

I took them, grinning. "Thanks, Alex." I looked at Mom and Dad, who were both observing us, and I wondered what they were thinking; probably that my life was a train wreck and wondering where Alex fit into it all. Honestly, I was shocked they even let him come over to visit their pregnant teenage daughter. They probably assumed there wasn't any worse trouble I could get into.

"Let's watch that movie," I suggested, nodding toward the living room.

"Thank you for letting me visit, Mr. and Mrs. O'Hara," he said gratefully. "You have a beautiful home."

"Thank you, Alex," Mom smiled. I was surprised she wasn't being stiff and cold.

"Just glad to see May coming out of her bedroom," Dad said. He winked at me.

It was awkward. I led the way to the living area and put my food and drink on the table so I could set up the movie, but Alex beat me to it. "I've got it," he insisted. "Get comfortable."

He knelt to insert the DVD. He had taken his shoes off at the door and was wearing mismatched socks: one blue and one green. I don't know why, but this detail was so endearing to me. "Nice socks," I teased with a tired grin.

He looked at me over his shoulder and laughed. "I didn't even notice. Just threw them on as I left."

Had he hurried over here? I was still taken aback by how he wanted anything to do with me, let alone how much he cared about my wellbeing. He stood up and shrugged out of his coat, laying it over the back of the couch before sitting next to me. He smelled good. Not like cologne; he just smelled good, like body wash and clothes fresh out of the dryer.

Then again, I could smell *everything* lately. Alex pressed a few buttons on the remote once the menu popped up, and soon the opening credits for the movie began to roll. He then opened my ginger ale by wrapping the bottom of his black t-shirt around the metal cap to twist it. It hissed and fog rolled out of the top.

"Potent stuff," I mused, taking it from him. "Thank you."

"Welcome," he smiled. "It's what the health food store guy recommended for morning sickness. Said it'll work better than the canned stuff."

I took a sip of it and the spice made my eyes water. It was warm going all the way down. But almost instantly, I could feel my stomach beginning to settle. "It's good."

"Good," he said, crossing his ankle over his knee as he settled back into the couch. "I'm really sorry you've been so sick."

"Me too," I sighed. "It's been rough."

He looked at me with caring eyes. "Have you decided for sure?"

I bit the inside of my lip. "I just can't do this any longer. I hope you don't think I'm weak for that."

"No," he insisted. "I think you're much stronger than you realize."

I exhaled shakily and rested my head against the back of the couch. "It's really good to know I have your support, even if you don't necessarily agree with my decision."

"I'll support you however you need me to, okay? I'm sure a lot of people think men shouldn't have an opinion in this matter, and I know I couldn't possibly understand what this is like. My personal convictions are strong and I hope you won't go through with this. I know you know I would be here all the time with ginger ale and cheesy movies if you decided to keep it. But if you don't? It's not going to change anything. I'll be here for you. That's how it should be. Nobody should be abandoned or neglected. This might be the hardest thing you ever do." He nudged my leg with his blue-socked foot. "I'm in your corner, okay?"

"Thank you, Alex. You don't know what that means to me."

He smiled and pulled a blanket off the arm of the couch to drape over us. "So, who's your favorite character?"

I pursed my lips, thinking as I tucked the blanket around me. "Wesley, of course. He's a total babe."

Alex laughed. "I think every guy on the planet wishes they could be as suave as Wesley. My favorite is Inigo Montoya."

"When I was a kid, I thought his name was Aluminum Foil," I laughed.

Alex cracked up. "Seriously? Aluminum Foil?" Then he quoted: "My name is Aluminum Foil. Prepare to die," accent and all.

I doubled over, laughing. Alex was dying too. Even his laugh was musical.

"I have a secret for you," he grinned when he stopped laughing. "But you have to promise not to tell."

I offered my pinky finger to him with a smile on my face. "Promise."

He wrapped his pinky around mine. "My full name isn't really Alexander Adair."

I lifted one brow, smirking. "Well, of course not. Most people have a middle name too."

He laughed. "Alexander *is* my middle name. See, when I was studying music in Portland, I also played at a lot of local venues for extra cash. I know this sounds weird, but I chose to go by my middle name because I felt like it suited me better."

"Oh?" I inquired, letting go of his pinky. "So what is your first name?"

He pulled his bottom lip between his teeth, peering at me intently. "Elijah. My full name is Elijah Alexander Adair."

"Elijah," I said, testing the name out. I studied his face. *God*, he was beautiful. "Funny. I think Elijah suits you better than Alex."

"Seriously?" he squinted, laughing. "Well, you can call me that if you want to. But Alex Adair will be my stage name if I ever get famous," he winked.

"Deal," I grinned. "I will keep your secret, *Elijah*."

Eventually our conversation died down and we became absorbed in the movie. We each had occasional commentary, like about how you could tell the Rodents of Unusual Size were just people in rat suits, and how terrible and amazing the acting was. It felt good to laugh with him, almost like there was hope for our friendship to be happy sometimes. By the time the movie was almost over, I had fallen asleep on his shoulder.

He woke me with a soft kiss on my forehead. "Hey," he whispered, tucking my hair away from my face.

I sighed contentedly and lifted my head. "Hey. Sorry."

"Don't be. Come on, I'll tuck you in."

"You'll tuck me in?" I asked with one eyebrow raised skeptically.

"Yep. No arguing." He stood and offered his hand to me, smiling.

I let him help me to my feet and together we went upstairs. Everyone was already in bed. He waited in my room while I brushed my teeth, and I blushed as I passed by him to climb beneath the covers.

He was pensive while he brought the blankets up around me, his eyes concentrated and thoughtful. "What is it?" I asked.

He looked at me and his expression softened. "Just wishing you weren't in so much pain."

"I'm really not," I insisted. "The ginger ale helped."

"That's not what I mean."

"Oh."

He knelt beside me and tilted his head, his blue hues twinkling in the lamp light. "Someday we will reflect on our pain as a stepping stone to our happiness. You'll see."

My chest ached. I wanted to again feel the way I felt when he kissed me. I wanted that happiness to come *now*. But it just wasn't the right time. And maybe it never would be, but I hoped for it. He filled a space in my life that I couldn't imagine another person ever filling. I couldn't imagine ever trusting another man the way I trusted him. "I can't wait for that day."

He smiled softly. "Goodnight. I'll let myself out. If you need anything, please call me."

"I will. Goodnight, Elijah."

"So it begins," he joked, bending down to kiss my forehead. When he was gone, I curled into a ball and cried myself to sleep. Not for me though. I was crying for him. I wanted so badly for this beautiful person to never feel pain again.

* * *

I DRANK THE REMAINDER of the ginger ale bottle the next morning, determined to go to school. Lying around had meant ample time to catch up on my assignments, but I didn't want to get behind. Once this pregnancy was terminated, I knew I would be able to get back into the swing of things. I just wished it would happen sooner rather than later.

After forcing down a few saltines, I was able to get showered and dressed to start my day. I found Grace sitting on my bed when I came out of the bathroom.

"Are you going to school?" she asked.

"Yes." I felt bad for neglecting her and her studies. "I promise I'll help you tonight."

"Don't worry about it," she murmured, walking over to my window to peer outside. The morning sun rays shone on her porcelain skin and made her look like an angel. She was so beautiful and delicate. So innocent. And I hadn't been there for her.

"I'm really sorry, Grace," I sighed. "I know it's been crazy lately, but I *will* help—"

"You're having an abortion tomorrow. The last thing you need is to worry about my studies."

There was a bitter edge to her tone and it cut me deep. "Grace, you know that won't change anything. It's just something I have to do."

"You don't *have* to do anything. When have you ever *had* to do anything in your life? You've always done what you wanted. Unlike me, who can't even have a sandwich before bed without asking."

"I didn't ask to be—" I stopped abruptly and hoped she wouldn't put the pieces together. How could I have been so careless? My blood boiled.

"You didn't ask to have sex?" she hissed. "Or you didn't ask to become pregnant? Because they kind of go hand in hand, May. What you're doing is a copout."

I had never heard her speak this way before. I had never even heard her raise her voice. And had her first statement not thrown me so far off guard, I would have congratulated her on showing a little emotion. But what she said felt like a noose around my throat, stifling any sort of response. "You have no idea what you're talking about," I said slowly.

"I know I'm disappointed. I know the only person I've ever really looked up to has proven to have zero integrity."

I exhaled sharply through my nose, feeling my nostrils flare in rage. I could have strangled her. I could have turned our house upside down and broken every single object within it. "Get out of my room," I hissed through my teeth. "And don't ever speak to me that way again. You don't know anything about this. You think you do, but you don't."

"Grow the hell up and take some responsibility," she snapped as she left.

The slamming door made my eyes slam shut. I grabbed my book bag and left without saying a word to anyone.

Twenty-Six

"SO HAVE YOU DECIDED?" Addison asked as she, Danika, and I sat in the cafeteria for lunch. They both looked at me expectantly, waiting for an answer.

I pushed my mashed potatoes around with my fork. "Yeah. I'm going through with it. My appointment is tomorrow."

Addison looked away, squinting in thought. Danika took the opportunity to respond. "If that's what you want to do, we're here for you."

"Thanks." I glanced around the room, absently scoping Tyler's whereabouts. I hadn't even realized this was a habit I had developed. "I was actually wondering if you guys would be willing to come with me? You'd just wait in the waiting room with my mom. I'm really scared and it would help if you were there."

"Of course," Danika confirmed. "Anything you need."

Addison was staring at her lunch tray and hadn't said a word. I sighed. "Addi? Will you come?"

Her eyes met mine and she looked like she could barely keep her head up. "I'm sorry." She shook her head. "I'm here for you and I love you, but I just don't think I can support this decision."

"Addison!" Danika snapped. "Are you kidding me? It's not like you're the one getting it done. She needs us."

She looked miserable, like what she was saying was causing her physical pain. "And I'll be there as soon as you leave that place.

Look, this hasn't been easy for me. I've been thinking about this all week. I know you didn't ask for this, but I can't convince myself I'm okay with taking an innocent life."

I stared at her in disbelief. "So you're taking a microscopic fetus's side over your best friend's?"

She dropped her fork. "No. I'm taking your side. You just don't see that right now."

"I can't believe you would be so selfish!" I snapped.

"Me?" she gaped, standing up the same time I did. "I'm not the one who is willing to kill a child for someone else's mistake!"

"*Mistake*? What, do you think he just *mistakenly* forced me to have sex? Or do you mean he mistakenly let the condom break?"

"You know that's not what I mean. Stop putting words in my mouth! I'm trying to help you."

"Go to hell, Addison! We're done."

The tables nearby fell quiet and I realized several groups had heard me, but I had no idea how much they heard. The only person I met eyes with was Tyler. His fists clenched on the table in front of him. I said nothing else, but I was sure by my expression he knew: he knew I was pregnant, and he knew it was his. That secret loomed in the gap between us; only he knew *who* I was talking about. I shook my head, wishing I could tell him I hated him. I wished I could make him suffer.

I avoided looking at anyone else as I took my tray to the trash and dumped my entire meal into it before throwing it onto the pile of dirty ones. I shoved through the double doors and made a beeline for the principal's office.

He looked at me, surprised by my abrupt entrance. "Can I help you, May?"

"I'm sick. I'm going home. And it's probably best that you know I'm not coming back."

He frowned, taking off his bifocals. "And why is that?"

I swallowed, quelling my nausea. "Would this be confidential?"

"Of course."

I lowered my voice. "I'm pregnant, but there are reasons I can't come back here. I'll be finishing school at home."

His thick, gray eyebrows lifted. "I see. But I will need parental confirmation of this. You can't just leave."

"Fine. I'm sure one of them will be here on Monday to sign me out, or whatever they have to do. Thanks, Mr. Greene." I didn't know what else to say, so I went to my locker for my things and left Ocean View for the last time.

* * *

I POUNDED ON THE DOOR of Elijah's bookstore after a few knocks. "Where are you?" I groaned in agony, cupping my hands over the window so I could peer inside. I hadn't seen his car in its usual spot, and he hadn't answered my calls. I broke down right then and there for the millionth time, it seemed.

"May?"

I turned around and saw him standing behind me with a bag of groceries. "I left school. For good, I mean," I stammered. "And you didn't answer your phone, and I was scared you hated me too."

He put the key in the lock while I rambled, hurriedly letting us inside. I almost wondered if he was ignoring me until he sat the bag down and pulled me into his arms. "Shhh . . ." he soothed. "How could I ever hate you?"

I gripped the back of his sweater in my hands, wishing I could disappear into him and never have to feel any of this again. Maybe if we were one person, our pain would have been easier to bear. But of course that was impossible. I was hysterical, sobbing so hard my knees threatened to give out.

He inhaled a deep breath and sang softly by my ear. I don't remember the words he sang, but I remember how quickly the sound of his voice calmed my weeping. He took my hand after a while and led me upstairs. I thought he was taking me to his piano, but he took me to his bedroom instead.

And the strange thing was, when he held up the covers for us to climb under them, I had not even a passing thought of being in Tyler's bed. I lay on his chest and he kept singing. Then he hummed until the last of my tears fell onto his shirt. He stroked my hair over and over. I was sure he didn't know this, but the strokes matched his breathing.

And even after I went home, I held onto that moment in my memory until morning dawned the next day.

* * *

MOM, DANIKA, AND I SAT in the waiting room at the clinic. I nervously tapped each of my fingertips against my legs while I waited for my name to be called. I wished one of them would say something, but I think they were just as nervous as me. Or maybe they just didn't know what to say. *I* didn't even know what to say.

"You alright, sweetheart?" a woman to my left asked. She had brown hair and tired brown eyes.

I smiled as politely as I could. "I think so."

She nodded. "I found out I was pregnant last week," she said. "My husband and I tried for over ten years to have a baby."

"Then . . . why are you here?" I asked, confused. I wondered if she had an affair.

"I have cancer. If I don't have the chemo, I'll definitely be too sick for it to work by the time the baby is here. But if I do have the chemo, I could live. And then maybe later, I could try again."

"I'm so sorry," I whispered. I felt terrible for judging her.

"Me too," she said, taking off her, gauzy, red scarf and putting it in the chair next to her. Sweat was beading on her forehead. "I wanted to try and have it, but then I found out he was cheating on me. He's gone now. It's just me and this baby I can't have." Her eyes welled up with tears as she touched her abdomen longingly. "But maybe someday, you know?" she said, smiling weakly at me.

"Yeah. Someday you will," I promised, hoping it would help her feel better at least.

She smiled thinly. "It's crazy how life works. You think you know what to do one moment, and the next you feel like there's no right answer." She patted my hand compassionately. "You look so young. You have your whole life ahead of you. It's never too late to embrace it."

I don't know why, but I felt safe to be a little open with her. "I wish I felt like that were true," I said softly, looking at her.

She fanned herself with a few abortion pamphlets. "You'll see. One day, it'll all make sense. It'll be crystal clear. I don't know your circumstance, but if there's any advice I can offer you, it's that I hope you'll remember this situation doesn't have to break you apart. You can choose to heal from it."

I knew she was only talking about my abortion, but somehow she was speaking to the rest of my heartache as well. "I had my whole future planned out. Now I just don't know." I glanced at my mother and found her and Danika talking quietly. I turned my attention back to the woman. "What are you going to do after this?"

"Well, I'll start my first aggressive round of chemotherapy. But the thing that really sucks about all of this is that chemotherapy can cause infertility. But, I supposed I can always adopt . . . if I live through this."

Tears stung my eyes. I hurt for her. "You will," I said firmly. "You'll live through it and you'll have the baby you've always wanted."

She looked at me for a long moment, a slow smile coming to her face. "I really hope you're right, sweetheart." She had a slight southern drawl. I could have imagined being friends with her in another time and place. I wondered what other wisdom she had to offer. "Thank you for that. And someday you'll have the baby you want, when the right time comes," she assured me.

"May O'Hara."

I looked at my mother and Danika. Mom tucked my hair behind my ear. "Do you want me to come in there with you?" she asked.

I shook my head. I needed to do this alone. "I'll be okay."

Her eyes watered. "Alright, baby."

She hadn't called me that since I was little. It was alarming. Was she worried something bad would happen?

I smiled at the woman I just met. She took my hand and squeezed it between both of hers, nodding encouragingly. I then turned my attention to the nurse waiting at the door and numbly got to my feet. She led the way down the hall to a door on the left, where she let me enter first. I stared at the table where the procedure would be performed.

"Have a seat for me," she said, taking a couple devices from a drawer. I sat on the table, hearing the paper crinkle under me. "It's okay to be nervous. Is there anything you'd like to talk about?"

"No." I shook my head and stared down at my hands.

"Alright. I just need you to sign this waver saying that any of your questions have been answered and you are still opting for a surgical abortion."

She handed me the clipboard and I scribbled my signature without even reading it. She took it from me and took my blood pressure and my temperature, scribbling things onto the next page on her clipboard. She then pricked my finger and took a sample of my blood.

All of it was happening so fast. I wanted to tell her to slow down; that I needed to get through this at my own pace. She was young; she didn't look much older than me. I wondered why she would choose to work in such a place as this. She weighed me, charted the number, then went through a few bottles of pills, dropping one of each in a little plastic cup. She filled a paper cup with water and handed both things to me. "These will help you relax. Go ahead and take them, and change into this gown here. I will be back with the doctor shortly."

I took the pills after she left. My hands shook as I threw the cup away and changed into the cotton gown, and then I sat on the table again to wait. Someone was crying next door. I waited and waited, pulse thrumming and hands shaking, until all at once, I felt my body grow heavy.

My nerves were deadening. I felt relaxed and calm, even though I knew I shouldn't have. I rested my elbows on my knees and continued to wait, hearing my own breath come in and out; in and out.

I was almost dozing when the door opened. "Hello, May," the doctor said flatly. He looked bored. Disinterested. "How are you feeling?"

"I'm okay," I answered. My voice sounded far away. I was nervous again, though I had no desire to move. "Would it be possible for a woman to see me?"

"I'm sorry, but no. Our other doctor is on maternity leave."

"Oh. Okay."

He sat on a stool and wheeled himself to my side. "Has anything changed since you filled out your information earlier this week?"

"No. It's all the same."

"Good. Would you like me to go over the procedure again with you?"

I shook my head. "I remember. Just . . . can you talk to me while you do it? So I know what's happening?"

"Sure. Go ahead and lie back for me, and put your feet in the stirrups." He draped a paper sheet over my legs. "We're going to begin with an ultrasound."

I did as I was told. My face burned when I positioned myself, and I fixed my eyes on the water-stained ceiling tiles as I braced for whatever was about to happen. I was freezing cold and sweating at the same time. I could just feel him looking at me, scrutinizing my most private area with clinical eyes.

The nurse picked up a probe of some kind and covered it with a clear, plastic barrier. She then squirted some gel onto it and handed it to the doctor. I clutched the sides of the table nervously. "Is this internal? I mean, are you going to . . . ?"

"Yes. When you're this early, it's best to get an internal view. Take a deep breath for me."

I inhaled and felt him push the probe into me. I winced, trying my best not to tense up. Deep pressure radiated in my lower abdomen. I screwed my eyes shut.

"Do you want to see the screen?"

"No," I said quickly, trying to breathe.

"Looks like you're about five weeks along, just as expected. I'm removing the probe now."

I exhaled, resting my clammy palm on my forehead.

"You're going to have to relax your legs a bit, May. I'm going to insert the speculum now. It'll be cold, but it will only be uncomfortable for a moment."

I nodded, though he couldn't see my head. I flinched when I felt the object he had forewarned me about, but immediately I felt lied to. It was painful. It was even more painful when it expanded, clicking several times. I whimpered into the crook of my arm and a tear slipped down my temple. The pressure was constant and I couldn't adjust to it.

"Good. Now I'm going to clean your vagina and cervix. Just take some deep breaths; I'll be gentle."

He kept talking but I barely heard him, my hearing fading in and out as I fought a sudden wave of nausea. "I'm going to throw up," I gasped, twisting to my side and sitting up at the same time. The nurse placed a pan under my chin, but nothing happened. I slowly lay back down and apologized, resisting the need to sob.

"I'm going to use a local anesthetic to numb your cervix now. You will feel some initial pinching, but after that you won't feel much of anything. Are you ready?"

"Yes," I choked. *Hurry. Just hurry up. Please!*

A sharp pain radiated through my abdomen and I groaned, sealing my hands over my face. I felt the nurse urging my legs apart, but it was almost impossible to let her spread them. "Wait. Wait! I need a minute!" I cried, wracked with sobs. The doctor stopped what he was doing and they both looked at me around the veil of my legs.

"It's not too late to turn back," he informed me. "You still have that option. The next step is dilating you, and after that I will have to finish the procedure."

Now

MY DAUGHTER LOVES to watch old videos of Addison dancing. We sit on the floor together, mesmerized by her youthful form as she floats across the stage on the TV. "Dah!" my girl squeals excitedly.

"Yeah, dancing," I answer, grinning. I stroke her soft curls. Addison leaps through the air and lands into a graceful tumble, coming back to her feet as though the whole move is effortless. Before I was raped, I went to every one of her recitals. I wonder where she would be today if she had been able to keep dancing.

"Maybe we should put her in dance lessons when she's old enough," Elijah says, joining us on the floor "She seems to really like it."

"Maybe," I agree, smiling at him. He has been writing music all morning and he looks tired, but energized at the same time. I lean toward him and kiss his lips. When we part, our daughter is watching us with a dimpled grin on her face.

Then

"YOU SURE THIS is what you want, sweetie?" the nurse asked, stroking my hairline on my forehead.

I nodded, forcing myself to breathe. "Yes. I'm sure. I'm just really scared."

"I know," she soothed. The doctor watched me as if he were waiting for the commercials of his favorite TV show to end. She gave him the go-ahead with a nod and he rolled back out of my view.

"Last injection," he said. I didn't feel this one. I heard metal objects shifting around, and then felt a slight throbbing deep inside me. "I'm dilating you. This will take a few minutes; just try to relax."

I imagined Addison dancing. I closed my eyes and remembered her recitals. I had gone to almost every single one. I didn't think about how she had abandoned me because of my decision. I just thought about the grace with which she had always moved and the way it had always made me feel like I was dreaming.

A switch was flipped and I heard the sound of quiet humming. "I'll begin the suction now, May," he told me.

A moment later, I heard the evidence of Tyler's offspring being pulled from my body. Sharp cramps tore through me and I writhed. The nurse did her best to hold me down.

Somehow, in that moment, I disappeared into a different reality: one where Elijah and I had no pain, and we could be happy together. One where the child I was pregnant with was his. One where none of this had ever happened. And I didn't come back to my nightmare until my mom and Danika came to get me. On my way out, I numbly picked up the scarf the woman from earlier had mistakenly left behind.

Twenty-Seven

I SLEPT ALL DAY. Danika went home at some point; I remembered her coming into my room to tell me goodbye. And now the sun was setting outside my window, amber rays glowing through my eyelids as I felt someone sit on my bed. Fingers brushed through my hair and I sighed, wincing when I felt the cramps I had been trying to sleep through. "Hey, Dewdrop," Dad said.

I looked up at him. His eyes were red and tired, much like they always were when he got off of work. But there was something else; something wrong. Mom came to kneel beside the bed and she wore the same look too. "I'm fine," I insisted, hoping they wouldn't dote on me. I didn't want that. I just wanted to get over all of this and move on.

Mom's lip quivered as she touched my arm. Her hand was ice-cold. "May," she began, pausing to clear her throat. "Something happened. Something terrible."

I sat up, propping myself on my elbows. I glanced back and forth between them, wondering who was going to fill me in. "What? What is it?"

Dad spoke first. "I was on the trauma floor this morning on my way upstairs. I passed by a room that was . . ." He looked at Mom and then back at me, the color dropping out of his face until he was white. "Addison had a car accident this morning, May."

I stared at him. The room around him spun. Pulling air in through my nose, I tried to swallow around the glue in my throat. "Is she alright?" my voice cracked.

Dad's eyes blinked rapidly. "She had a massive brain injury. The bleeding on her brain was—"

"Did she live?" I cut him off sharply, grasping onto his arms.

He swallowed. "I'm sorry, baby. She passed away before I could do anything to stop the hemorrhage."

"No," I whispered. Dad pulled me close and rocked me. I could hear Mom crying. But for some reason, my tears didn't come. It didn't seem real. It was as if it were just another part of this nightmare I was living. Surely if I tried hard enough, I could wake up.

Wake up . . . wake up!

When would it stop? The pain; the loss.

Would it ever?

All at once it was as if a jolt of electricity had hit my body and I began to weep inconsolably. "Why?" I groaned, dissolving helplessly in my dad's arms like a child. I couldn't breathe. I had no control over my body except to fall apart, my head falling back against his arm as I wailed. Mom kissed my forehead, clasping my hand between hers. And this went on until the sun had given up and my room was dark, and the only light illuminating it was that of my carousel on my dresser. Lights danced around the walls like fireflies, lulling me again to sleep once my body had no more strength to cry.

I slipped into a dream. Addison and I were fighting all over again.

* * *

"ALEX, I KNOW YOU really want to check on her, but it's just not a good time."

My eyes fluttered open and I looked for him, quickly realizing the window was open and the voices were coming from outside. Dad was sleeping beside me.

"I'm just really worried about her, Mrs. O'Hara."

"I know you are. I'll tell her you stopped by."

No. I wanted to see him. I slipped out of bed and went to the window, catching myself against the sill. He closed the door of his car, leaving me no chance to call his name. I sank to the floor and brought my knees to my chest, sobbing quietly into my bent arms. Eventually I rested my head against the wall and took a few steeling breaths: in through my nose, out through my mouth, slowly gaining control of myself. I reached for my purse and dug my phone out of it so I could call him.

That's when I saw Addison's text messages and voicemail waiting to be opened.

I shook as I tapped the screen.

> *Addison: I'm so sorry, May. I don't agree with what you've decided to do, but that doesn't mean I don't love you and want to support you regardless. I just can't go to the clinic. I hope you can forgive me.*

I groaned with an agonized cry. Of course I forgave her. I just wanted her back. I opened the next text.

> *Addison: I'm heading to your house. I'll see you there when you get home from your appointment. I want to be here for you, May. I love you.*

I dropped my phone. She was on the way to my house when she had her accident.

I got off the floor and ran out of my room, hearing my dad call my name. I ran past my mom in the kitchen. I ran to the sidewalk where I sprinted on bare feet until my lungs gave out and I collapsed onto a stranger's lawn. I tried to suck in a breath. Blood stained the inside of my pajama pants as my abdomen twisted painfully.

A moment later, Dad lifted me into his arms and carried me home.

Twenty-Eight

WHEN I WAS A KID, I asked my dad what it meant to die. Being the scientifically-minded individual he was, he told me exactly what it meant: that your heart stops beating and your body no longer functions. He said your soul, the part that made you who you were, went on to somewhere better. That wasn't the doctor speaking, of course. I don't think my dad even believed in heaven or hell. I just think he wanted that pill to be easier for a six-year-old to swallow.

I didn't even know what I believed. Most people have at least an idea of what they consider to be true by the time they're in their teens, but I had never considered it. Maybe it was because I heard about death in such a black and white manner my entire life. There were no stories of white lights or angels singing.

But I really, *really* wanted to believe the angels were singing today.

"You look beautiful," Mom said behind me as I finished tying my hair back in front of my floor-length mirror. I wore a knee-length, black dress with a pair of faux pearl earrings Addison had given me for my thirteenth birthday. Who cared if I looked beautiful? I didn't. But I thanked her anyway, because I knew she was just trying to communicate with me. The last three days had been the worst of my life, and I hadn't spoken to anyone. Not my parents, not Danika . . . not even Elijah.

I picked up the scarf the woman had worn to the clinic and draped it around my neck. It smelled like her: flowery and clean. It didn't go with my ensemble, but that didn't matter. All these years later, I still don't know why I carried that scarf around with me for so long. Sometimes it felt as if I were punishing myself, and other times it felt as if I were paying respect to the woman who might have lived by sacrificing her desperately wanted child's life. Maybe I was really just paying respect to that child.

I think it was a little bit of all these things. That scarf reminded me of Addison. It reminded me of death and it reminded me of life. It reminded me I had survived, and on that particular day, it actually felt like a punishment.

I stared quietly out the window while Dad drove all of us to the chapel where the service would be held. I expected it to be a big gathering because Addison was loved by so many people; the dance community, especially. And I was right. Upon pulling into the parking lot, it was quickly apparent the chapel would be full to the brim.

I was glad. She deserved it.

I took my seat in the second row to the front. The old pew creaked a little when my family sat next to me; voices were hushed and Mr. and Mrs. Flood were sitting on the front row, crying in each other's arms. I could have reached out and touched them. Mrs. Flood repositioned her head on her husband's shoulder and her mascara-stained eyes opened, meeting mine. She extended her arm and took hold of my hand, and that was when I broke.

"I'm so sorry," I whispered tearfully. "I'm so sorry."

"I know, honey," she answered, squeezing my hand one last time before facing the front of the church. The pastor had taken his place behind the pulpit.

I didn't hear a word he said. All I could do was stare at the glossy black casket in front of him, trying to understand how I had just seen Addison the other day and now she was lying lifeless within it. I tried to cry quietly; I really did. I didn't want to be a distraction. I wanted Addison to have the attention she deserved.

Someone slipped into the pew beside me and tugged up on the thighs of his slacks before sitting down. I realized it was Elijah when his hand slipped into mine. I grasped onto him as though he were the only thing keeping me from disappearing. We looked at each other and the light coming through the stained glass windows splashed his eyes with vibrant colors. He smiled sadly at me and let go of my hand to drape his arm around my shoulders. I rested my face on his chest and tried not to stain his suit coat with my tears.

Bible verses were read. I stared at the window that was shining over her casket; it depicted a dove in flight, carrying a branch of some kind in its mouth. I had heard somewhere that the dove was the symbol of peace. For a moment I hoped that Addison was at peace, and then I realized she hadn't been miserable to begin with. She hadn't been riddled with cancer. She hadn't suffered at the hands of a murderer. Addison was as bright as the light shining through that window, full of life and passion. And now she was gone. She was gone because of me.

I leapt out of the pew and brushed by Elijah to escape, running down the aisle toward the exit. I heard Danika call my name, but I kept running. My heels thudded with every step until I burst through the double doors and disappeared into the wooded area behind the chapel.

Grabbing onto a tree, I sank to my knees and leaned against it to catch my breath. The bark dug into my arm and the cold air bit my skin, but I barely felt it. I hadn't felt anything in over two weeks except for the churning sea in my heart. The muscle itself hurt so badly in my chest that I wished I could rip it out, but it continued to thud with repeated reminders of what I had lost and the damage I had done.

"What have I done?" I whispered brokenly into the quiet, damp forest. For the first time, I felt the burden of two lives lost: Addison's and my child that would never be.

Twenty-Nine

THE TEN MONTHS following Addison's death were overwhelming. It was as if the world were spinning around me and I was powerless to stop it or even slow it down.

I was back to my old self in ways, but I wasn't alright. There was this constant weight on my shoulders I couldn't seem to shrug off. My nightmares were far more intermittent than they had been, but I wished they would go away altogether. I wished I could understand why this had taken over my life. Was it normal to still be hurting like this ten months later?

From the rape, I mean. And what I did afterward. I knew I would never stop hurting over Addison.

I wished I could tell her I was thankful for everything she did, and for the ways she tried to help me. I knew I would always regret the way I reacted when she said she couldn't support my decision. I just hoped that somehow she knew how much I really loved her. I told her that at least once a month when I visited her in the cemetery, but I wished she could hear it. Who knows? Maybe she did.

I might have been crazy, but sometimes I wished I had kept the baby, or at least given it up for adoption. Somehow I thought it might have given me some kind of hope that something good could come out of what happened. But it was done. I would never know what might have been.

Even though I was still in this fog of depression, I still managed to graduate with honors. And I was proud when I took the stage to accept my diploma. Just a few students down the line, *he* stood looking everywhere but at me. I was thankful for that. I was thankful he never talked to me again after the day he asked if I would be pressing charges. Honestly? I think I might have strangled him.

I was angrier than I used to be. Not just at Tyler, but in general. Elijah had to talk me down a few times, saying I was losing sight of the good things in life. He was so good to me. I know *he* was what was good in life. I don't know what he saw in me, or why he chose to stick around when I could do nothing to contribute to our relationship . . . but for some reason, he did. He always said I would be alright. I tried so hard to believe him.

He told me he loved me for the first time about six months after Addison died. I had never seen his eyes sparkle that much. It was as if they had captured every star twinkling in the sky. His confession flooded me with a sense of peace, but at the same time, I was frightened. I didn't say it back. I think most guys would have given up on me then and there, but he just held me and said it was okay.

It took a while, but I knew I was ready to say it back. And I went to his apartment for that very purpose.

* * *

ELIJAH OPENED THE DOOR to his upstairs apartment before I knocked, surprised to see me standing there. He had given me a key to the shop a few months before after hiring me to work on weekdays after school, so my arrival wasn't completely out of my norm, but I usually called him first. "Sorry, I probably should have let you know I was coming over . . ."

"Are you kidding?" he grinned, stepping over the threshold to wrap me up against him.

I inhaled his scent deeply, fisting the back of his black t-shirt. He never denied me from stopping by on the weekend to see him. I felt his fingers stroke my hair all the way down to my waist. He loved to twist it around his fingers.

After a moment, he pulled back and looked at me, a content smile on his lips. "I missed you," he said.

"You saw me last night," I argued with a smirk, still holding onto his waist.

"Mmmm. Too long." He brushed his lips over mine and my body tingled all the way to the tips of my toes. Lately, I had butterflies. They had taken a while to find their way into my stomach, but they were there now, fluttering every time he looked at me; every time he kissed me, touched me, or told me he loved me.

I grinned, deepening the kiss, breathing him in. I wrapped my arms around his neck and stood on my tiptoes, trying to get closer. I heard him moan softly. The pull between us was more powerful than I ever imagined it could be. But he always gently and respectfully broke the kiss so we wouldn't go any further. He knew about my desire to wait for marriage; sometimes I thought he respected it more than I did. I still had trouble believing there was any point in saving my virginity for marriage after it had already been taken. And there were many times when I would have happily given him what was left of me. And even though I could have felt rejected when he didn't take it, I only felt more loved.

Elijah loved all of me, even the broken parts I was ashamed of.

"Where were you going?" I asked breathlessly.

He looked at me, confused.

"When I came to your door, you seemed to be going somewhere," I explained.

"Oh. Just downstairs to do some organizing." His thumbs gently rubbed my waist where his hands were resting. I wondered if he knew what that did to me. "Are you alright?"

I knew he was asking because I showed up unannounced. "I'm fine. Come on, I'll help you."

He grinned and took my hand, leading the way downstairs. We went to a shelf he had recently built to house books about Oregon, something locals frequently asked about. I sat on the floor and began going through the boxes, daydreaming as I looked at their beautiful covers. All of them portrayed a different place: Salt Creek Falls, Newport Beach, the Tamolitch Pool; the list went on and on. Sometimes I forgot I lived in such a beautiful state.

"What are you thinking about?" he asked, standing over me as he took books one by one to be alphabetized.

I frowned thoughtfully. "Just that sometimes I forget what's around me. Even our town is beautiful. I guess I have stopped taking it in lately."

"It is," he agreed. "It took me a while to adapt to it after living in Portland, but now I don't think I would ever want to live in a big city again."

I stared at his tattered, black Converse shoes for a moment, noticing that his shoelaces were frayed. I had forgotten that his shoes looked brand new when I first met him. I don't know why, but I reached out and touched the double knot, knowing it hadn't been untied in months.

He knelt next to me and lifted my chin with his fingers. "What is it?" he asked softly, looking into my eyes.

"I love you," I blurted. My eyes instantly swam with tears. I shook my head quickly, blinking. "I mean . . . I didn't mean to tell you that. Now, I mean. I was going to tell you later, at dinner or something. Somewhere romantic, I guess? That was really strange timing . . ."

His eyes watered as a grin slipped across his face. He yanked me into his arms and we tumbled to the floor with me lying on his chest. He pushed his hands up into my hair and brought my face to his for a gentle kiss. "Our timing has always been perfect," he whispered.

Thirty

FOUR YEARS HAVE PASSED. After my abortion, I developed an obsession with hearing the abortion stories told by other women. I found that pregnancy caused by rape is significantly rare compared to pregnancy caused by casual, unprotected sex. I learned that it isn't all that unusual to regret one's decision to abort. And I have found that most women who claim not to regret their abortion still have mixed emotions beneath the surface.

For me? I still dream about him. And no, I was never far along enough to learn his gender. But I know what I dream.

Tyler raped me. He took what wasn't his, and his actions caused a domino effect of painful obstacles in my life. I once explained my dreams to a psychologist and she informed me that regardless of the way in which the child was conceived, it's almost impossible for most of us not to recognize that we once bore a human life. To this day, I can't wrap my mind around *why* I regret ending that life. But I do. And I know it's not the same for every woman, and my feelings are mine alone, but I think it's pretty safe to say I'm not the only one who secretly misses what might have been.

In the year following my rape, I finally gained the courage to tell my parents and Grace the truth. And though my mother threatened to do everything in her power to ensure Tyler was convicted, in the end, she knew nothing could be done. Since I neglected to report it, and due to the lack of evidence, there was no way to prove it. So all they could do was grieve. And all I could do was try to show them I would be alright.

My relationship with Danika crumbled during that year as well. When it came down to it, I knew I held no resentment toward her for that night. But she couldn't look at me without blaming herself, and I couldn't look at her without remembering. We check on each other now and then though, with a phone call here or there. She just graduated from the University of Oregon with a degree in interior design, and has already been hired at a design firm in Seattle. She married an accountant, and she has a baby on the way.

Everyone has moved on. I'm still trying to do the same.

I have carried that scarf around for years. I don't know what became of the woman who owned it, but it reminds me now that I am alive. I am somehow functioning, even in the midst of nightmares and the grieving of my best friend. Some days it feels like I will never let her go. Other days it's like she's still here and just a phone call away.

I found out I was pregnant on the anniversary of Addison's death. It only seemed fitting that my daughter should be named after her. The day she was born, she was placed in my arms and for the first time in so long, I cried because I was happy.

Elijah has been my rock. It hasn't mattered that I've been broken. He has slowly but surely been supporting me as I repair my wings. He's not my savior though. Through him, I have learned how *I* am the only one who can repair myself.

My family took him in with open arms four years ago. We married two years later. Adair Books flourished after much trial and error, and we lived in that little upstairs apartment up until a month ago. Now we are the proud owners of a beach condo. And I came around to it late, but I am in my first year of college. I am determined to be a doctor like I always wanted.

I also write. I write to heal. I write to process things. Writing has become such a huge part of my identity that I don't think I can ever be separate from it.

The living room is packed with guests, most of which are from my dad's side of the family. Dad is sitting on the couch with Mom, laughing at something someone said. Grace is standing in the corner of the room with her boyfriend, James. She and I have never really been close, but we understand and love each other. We share rare moments where it almost feels like we're best friends, but the truth is I really don't have friends anymore.

The doorbell rings and I leave the living room to answer it, expecting another guest. Instead I find the UPS man. He holds out a padded envelope to me and has me sign his electronic pad. I tell him goodbye and look at the name on the package: *Elijah Alexander Adair*.

He isn't here right now. He's outside on the grassy cliff with Addison, letting her see the ocean. Sometimes it is the only thing that eases her when she is upset.

I hook my finger under the top of the envelope and tear it open. Inside is a stack of papers. I pull them out and notice the name at the top: *Virtuoso Recording Co.*

My heart skips as I scan the lines below. I read them out loud. "Mr. Adair, I am pleased to inform you that our label would like to represent you. Please read the following . . . ."

I rush out the door. "Elijah!" I call, clutching the papers to my chest so they don't blow away in the wind.

He turns around and grins at me, bouncing Addison gently on his hip. The grass sways up to his thighs. "Hey," he says. "What is that?"

"You did it!" I beam, turning the stack of papers around so he can see them. I see his eyes light up in disbelief. "You really did it."

He kisses me fiercely, pulling me against him with his free arm. The wind whips around, blasting us with cool, salty, coastal air. The feeling is magical. "Your smile is so beautiful," he tells me when we part. I know I don't smile enough for him. The way he says this, though I know it isn't intentional, makes me regret not finding more reasons to make him happy.

But I know that's not why he wants me to smile; I know it's because he wants *me* to be happy.

I touch his cheek, shaking my head in amazement. "I'm so proud of you. I'm so proud to be your wife."

I can tell that something inside of him is soothed by me saying that. His beautiful eyes soften and he leans into my touch. "I love you, May. I've always loved you."

"I love you too," I answer with all my heart.

He grins and looks at Addison. She smiles back at him, a mirror reflection of her father. "Come on. Let's go tell everyone," he says excitedly, reaching for my hand.

I take it, but I stop him. "I need a moment. Will you wait until I come inside to tell them?"

"Of course." He kisses my forehead. "We'll be waiting."

I watch him go into the house, turning around to face the ocean once he's gone. The wind stings my eyes as I observe the scene before me. Storms brew in the distance; lightning crashes over the ocean in far away flashes. The tide roars with angst, stirring the shore with crashing waves. It's been so long since I thought about who I am, and who I was before those fateful two weeks. I have been holding onto them, afraid to let go for fear I might have no identity at all. I had thought that choosing to end my pregnancy was the only choice I would ever have to make; that everything else—all of my pain—was secondary. I had thought it was all just part of a burden I had to bear.

Elijah has never let me count on him for my healing. He has always pushed me to discover my own strength; to believe in myself enough to take flight once again. But I'm scared. I'm so scared that if I try, I will discover that my wings have healed all wrong. What if I fall from the sky and land in the ocean, only to be destroyed by the tide all over again?

I release a breath. "What am I supposed to do?" I ask the stormy horizon, slipping my hands into the back pockets of my jeans. I feel my phone and pull it out.

The voicemail. It still sits tucked away in the same phone I have never gotten rid of, because to do so would mean throwing away Addison's last words to me.

Tears slip from my eyes as I slowly flip it open. I know she would have wanted me to listen to it, but I have never had the strength to. I know I never will. And so, I press the button that will play it, bringing the phone to my ear. Addison's voice rings through over the static of wind; she always drove with her windows down.

"Remember when we were kids and we promised to always be honest with each other? I wasn't honest with you at first. Not completely anyway. When you first told me you were considering ending this pregnancy, I told you I would support you, but I didn't tell you how strongly I feel about this. But that being said . . . I know you probably already had it done. Your appointment started half an hour ago. And because it's probably already done, nothing I am saying matters in terms of helping you decide. So instead, I want you to know you'll be okay." Her voice shook with emotion. When she spoke again, she was crying. "I want you to know this doesn't change how amazing I think you are; how strong I *know* you are. Having an abortion won't fix your pain, and I know you know that you'll always have memories tied to it as well. I don't know if you'll ever regret it, but I know you won't be unaffected by it." She paused, collecting her thoughts.

"You didn't have a choice in what Tyler did. You had a choice about whether or not to end your pregnancy. But that's not the only choice you'll ever have. You can heal, May. Forget everything anyone has tried to tell you and just remember that ultimately *you* decide how your story goes. I might not know much about loss, but I know you. And I know that you'll be okay if you don't let any of this hold you back. I'll always be here to support you, no matter what. I love you."

I stare at the dark horizon, my hair whipping behind me. My tears flow endlessly, and they likely always will. "You'll always be here," I whisper, somehow knowing it's true. "Thank you, Addi."

A gust of wind hits me so hard that it almost knocks me over. My scarf comes unwound from my neck and begins to float away. I gasp, catching it before it's gone.

I watch it flap in the air as if it is desperately trying to escape. And I know: whether I heal or not, and whether I fly or fall, it is my choice to make. And my choice is the one thing that can never be stolen from me.

I close my eyes, and with a breath of release, I open my hand.

Acknowledgments

Where do I even begin? Thank you, God, for carrying me through.

Thank you to my dear friends and family who allowed me to vent and struggled with me through this book. Thank you for helping me wrestle with the parts that were almost impossible to write.

Thank you Jill Weinstein and J.C. Wing, for polishing my work. You're amazing!

Readers, I so appreciate your support and devotion to my writing. Words will never be able to express how thankful I am for you.

For more resources, visit: www.rainn.org

Made in the USA
Columbia, SC
12 January 2022